TOWER OF DEATH: THE ADVENTURES OF SCARLET AND BRADSHAW, VOLUME 3

The Complete Cases of The Mongoose

BY JOHNSTON MCCULLEY

The Girl and the People of the Golden Atom

BY RAY CUMMINGS

*The Gray Dragon: The Adventures
of Peter the Brazen, Volume 2*

BY LORING BRENT

The Golden City

BY RALPH MILNE FARLEY

*The House of Invisible Bondage: The Complete
Cabalistic Cases of Semi Dual, the Occult Detector*

BY J.U. GIESY AND JUNIUS B. SMITH

*The Scrap of Lace: The Complete Cases
of Madame Storey, Volume 1*

BY HULBERT FOOTNER

The Devil-Tree of El Dorado

BY FRANK AUBREY

*The Firebrand: The Complete
Adventures of Tizzo, Volume 1*

BY MAX BRAND

*Marching Sands and The Caravan of the
Dead: The Harold Lamb Omnibus*

BY HAROLD LAMB

TOWER OF DEATH

THE ADVENTURES OF SCARLET
AND BRADSHAW, VOLUME 3

THEODORE ROSCOE

ILLUSTRATED BY

M. LINCOLN LEE
JOHN R. NEILL
GEORGE WERT

STEEGER BOOKS • 2019

TABLE OF CONTENTS

THE LAST BATTLE

Africa, the Dark Continent, hides many a mystery; but no other so astounding as the weird doom that threatened Bradshaw's expedition and the lonely outposts they visited after the war

PROLOGUE

TELL US A story of the war! Make it gripping and different; but wild with the crackle of guns and brave with the valor of fighting men. Give us a story of the soldier, the man who gave all for the love of his country. Give us a story of battle. Tell us a story of the war....

All right, I'll tell you one. I'll tell you the story that Bradshaw, the Kelantan naturalist, told the British government agent and me one night when we were left to the veranda of the Colony Club in Pahang and the crickets were chirping. A stern British cruiser was standing out to sea, leaving a sullen smoke smudge against the sunset beyond the Straits, and the thin, clear strain of a bugle call drifted from across the water.

"Reminds me of the old days," the British agent chuckled. "That bugle. I was in the rumpus on the Somme. A gory hell. I say, Bradshaw, you were in the service at first with Allenby, weren't you? Did you see any fighting?"

"Fighting?" The naturalist spread his fingers, reflectively. "Yes, some of that campaign was pretty warm. It's not odd the bugle on that gunboat should recall the war to me, too. But I wasn't thinking of the scrap in that quarter. I was thinking of a battle that... Listen. Did I ever tell you I fought in the last battle of the war? The last terrible charge?

"Say, that *was* a fight! Of all the battles of the war I think it was the fiercest. A wildcat fight. And the queerest, too. Such a clogged blind courage, such a faith to duty and heroism and

1

bravery in the face of staggering odds I've never seen anywhere before or since. What a charge! And I don't mean the fighting of October, '18." Bradshaw yanked out his calabash and lit it as he might have touched off a bomb. "I mean the battle that will never get the spot in history books it deserves. The very last fight of the war."

That it happened in an African jungle where lions padded through spear grass, where snakes the hue of a rainbow slept, deadly, in warm black pools, where weird birds called and black men's drums beat late in the jabberwock gloom—that it happened deep in Africa makes no difference, after all. You wanted a different war story, and Bradshaw told one. He puffed on his calabash and watched something far away take form in the uncoiling lariat of smoke.

"I'll tell you about that last battle," he said.

And he did:

CHAPTER I

A STRANGE SAFARI

TEN YEARS AGO—JANUARY, 1920, to be exact—I dropped down to Dar-es-Salaam with a letter from the Natural History Society in my pocket which commissioned me to join the International Tanganyika Expedition. I'd been a little chary about taking the assignment, for it came suddenly and the only thing I knew about the business was that the expedition intended to hunt gorillas.

But the minute I joined up I was glad, for they'd certainly placed me in a mighty good outfit. I was aware that trekking African bush on the trail of the giant gorilla was no job for lilies and amateurs. The gorilla country had a habit of reducing a man into a skeleton that bleached in the sun. Some of the hills in there were the wildest spots on earth, scarcely mapped

He just sat like something in flint,
quiet and aloof as an image

and known to few white men. And the native inhabitants were suspected of enjoying human flesh on their bills of fare—that old Congo delicacy so cheerless to contemplate.

But if anybody could brave that demon country, the men in this Tanganyika Expedition could do it. International? You might have thought we were setting out to build the Tower of Babel. If we had been I'll wager we'd have stolen a march on the Scriptures and finished the job. But not one of us in the party swore the same sort of oath.

There was Langle de Lanrezac, the little Walloon Belgian, naturalist from Antwerp. There was Gustav Garonne from the Paris Jardins. The two famous elephant hunters, Francesco Carpetsi of Italy and Feofan Filipich, the Russian, were with us. There was the young British sportsman and big game hunter, Peter Firestone, outfitted by the British Museum. And last we were joined by the old collector, Hilmar von Letterbeck, sent from Berlin. Every man named was a collector and hunter of note, and von Letterbeck had won world-wide acclaim the year before by his daring explorations in the South Polar wilderness.

You can see it was an unusual party that set out across Tanganyika for Lake Kivu and Mount Karisimbi where the gorillas were known to be. I was thinking it was going to be hard on those apes when we arrived. With our *safari,* the seven of us looked nothing so much as a punitive army corps, dressed in military khaki, pith helmets, automatics belt and rifles under arm. We carried neat little Kirby guns for smaller game and hung our saddles with those monster .475 elephant guns that can drop a bullet through a brick-wall. The native chiefs went down like smitten caterpillars when they saw us coming up the trail.

Well, things went beautifully the first days of the trek. Everybody seemed to be in high spirits, enjoying the country and the company and the job, having a fine time. Everybody, that is, save the old German, von Letterbeck. Our first night out, the rest of us were pouring long drinks together, getting acquainted, comparing notes. You know how it is on the trail with a camp fire to crackle in your ears and a pipe to smoke in your fist and a good adventure ahead. You find it easy to be friendly under an open sky and owning a common interest.

But the old collector from Berlin wasn't friendly. I thought to myself I'd never seen a sourer soul. You know the Prussian of the old, pre-war régime? Austere Teuton face with Kaiser Wilhelm mustaches standing grim guard on either side of a stern nose. Brush-cut hair. A chin and mouth set like guns. A neck stiff as a ramrod and eyes that seemed to push you off the curb.

You know the sort of German who owned a mind like a book on mathematics, the Junker who was iron Jehovah to his family, the *Generalstabsoffizier* who'd been in military school since the age of three, never forgot a rule, and goose-stepped his men till their spines shrieked? You recall the type? Then you know old Hilmar.

OLD VON LETTERBECK would ride along our jungle trail

the way a Hohenzollern used to ride down Unter den Linden. Never taking those metal blue eyes off the path ahead. Never blinking in the sun. He didn't join in our conversation around the camp fires; just sat like something in flint, occasionally offering a cold smile or correcting a technicality, quiet and aloof as an image. Up and to bed like a clock, he kept his outfit packed like a soldier's, his horse in trim like a general's, his black boys stepping like orderlies. The nearest thing to an automaton I'd ever seen.

But most of all it was his somber silence that pushed a man away from him. The farther into the hinterland we rode, the more von Letterbeck drew himself into an impenetrable shell. I had a feeling that the man quite hated the country we were in and would never have come on the expedition if his Fatherland had not sent him. But of course, in his deep silence, he never said anything about it. Finally he even refused to join the circle at the camp fire; took to riding off by himself at dusk and making a solitary, two-hour excursion in the starlit darkness.

The rest of us, tolerant and trying to be friendly, were somewhat concerned.

"It's bad country to wander alone, the land we are entering," de Lanrezac, the Belgian, pointed out. "Perhaps it would be better if Herr von Letterbeck did not ride off by himself. *Mais oui!* The blacks are not civilized in here, and farther in, along that Urindi border, there are tribes very wild."

"Some of those bloody savages live in swamps and hills like poison," young Firestone observed. "I've heard how they'll stay hidden for years at a time, some of those tribes. White men go in there and aren't heard of again." The Englishman was mildly respectful, but gave warning with some concern. "You better be careful, von Letterbeck."

Sitting in his saddle, old Hilmar von Letterbeck did not appear to listen. But he looked down with something like an appreciative smile.

"*Danke schön*, my friends, but I enjoy the ride. I am always careful." And he patted the barrel of the big .475 at his side, as he cantered off under the early stars.

It was not for Hilmar von Letterbeck to be careless or show fear. His stern Prussian face never altered a muscle when our expedition encountered the first of those astounding episodes that were soon to string taut wires of terror, unseen, through the jungle glooms. Old Hilmar von Letterbeck did not bat an eye at something which made the hair prickle on my own neck as it had never prickled before—something so weird and terrifying as to make us clutch tight our rifles and ride with fingers on trigger.

I'VE BEEN in some pretty thick jungle bottoms in my day, but never anything to match the country we entered when we left the White Friar's Mission at Ugala and pushed up the river toward the north end of Tanganyika Lake. The British East African government officials had supplied us with the finest of trail maps and instructions, but the swampy black terrain we crossed was almost roadless and much of the path had to be hacked out by our boys. We were taking a roundabout way to our destination, almost breaking a trail, but that was part of our objective and we hoped to gain good specimens other than gorilla.

De Lanrezac picked the route, and Peter Firestone acted as main guide. Gustav Garonne claimed to have trekked the territory before, and the two elephant trackers, Filipich and Carpetsi, seemed to know it like a book. To my surprise, von Letterbeck also professed a knowledge of the country, speaking the native dialects and often advising this or that course. Firestone and the others had hunted through there before, but I was surprised that the old German should be familiar with the land.

It was wilderness jungle, all right. Our trail cut through tunnels roofed with mats of foliage, riotous vine, dank vegetation atangle. Bogs of inky muck where serpents slid. Dark pools alive with crocodile. Fens abounding with wild boar and savage hog. There were birds of every odd description, plant life of rarest variety, leopard and lion and deadly fly. Add tropic fever and tropic sun and natives who'd never seen a white man before, and you get some idea of the road we traveled. A naturalist's paradise and any man's hell.

And our little party was going a bit strange, too. Von Letterbeck's odd conduct, his weighted silence, the way he stood aloof and rode off by himself, buried himself in our midst, was beginning to pall. You know how one link can affect the whole chain. Von Letterbeck was like that. Naturally, the rest of us thrown together for a period of time in a strange locale got together and made companionship. The old German refused to open up at all.

"I get a blasted strange impression the old flintlock has something heavy on his mind," Firestone observed that night at camp fire. "Every day he grows more silent, draws farther back into himself. One might as well try to make friends with the Sphinx."

"I talk to him," Garonne complained, tugging his black French beard, "and he says 'yes' or 'no,' that is all. I said to him how I enjoyed his volume on polar exploration. It was a good book, I said. He only nodded. He is like a being of rock, that one."

Carpetsi, the Italian, twisted his mustache. "The German is a master at tracking and hunting. Did you see him shoot that boar, yesterday? A marksman. But a man the most silent. *Per Bacco!* I think he has traveled always alone in solitary lands and has forgotten friendliness."

"I think," remarked the gaunt and red-bearded Filipich, "that our German comrade suffers great hate for something. Yesterday dawn I was with him when we rode to top that hill, and the land lay before us and we sighted our first view of the lake. I was about to say what a beautiful scene, when I caught a glimpse of von Letterbeck. Saint Mitrophane! There was something in his eye that chilled me! Something frightening. An eye of cold hatred. It closed my mouth and I said nothing to him."

CHAPTER II

OUTPOST OF SILENCE

SO WE GOSSIPED and wondered about the man so much a stranger in our midst; and then we won something else to talk about. You bet we did! We camped one night on the crest of a steep hill, and Tanganyika Lake was a gleaming watery jewel below us. Journey's end was near. A hundred miles' farther up the shore and we would cross the Urindi border, traverse a territory under Belgian-British mandate and see Lake Kivu and Karisimbi. We'd made a long, difficult trek without mishap; shipped back some splendid specimens—the pygmy hippo I had bagged that day on the river was one of my finest—and the trip was promising high success.

Around the fire that night we drank long toasts to the gorillas we all hoped to collect for our respective museums. Even old von Letterbeck wandered up to hoist a glass with us before saddling his pony for his inevitable solitary excursion. But he did not stay to yarn with us; jammed on his sun helmet and rode off by himself, stiff as starch; and the rest of us, dog-tired, turned in early. Next morning we were to hit the lake shore where Firestone claimed the trail was fine, and breakfast time would find us at a little British outpost where we could reprovision our *safari*.

We turned in with a thump of tomtoms in our ears. Our black boys were enjoying lion steak and a fire in their camp farther up the trail, and the echo of the drums and stamping feet pulsed like the heart of Africa, itself. I don't know why, but as I lay in my blankets that night, sleep heavy on my eyes, the Russian hunter snoring on one side of me and the little Frenchman snoring on the other, I was assailed by a sense that something was going to happen.

The last thing I saw that night was a patch of gloom painted dimly scarlet by the smoky fire of our black porters. The last thing I heard was the weird, barbaric chant of their dance, the tuneless throb of their drums. I was conscious that von Letterbeck had ridden out of the darkness, dismounted, and gone to his blankets with an oppressive sigh.

Then it was a morning of blatant, hot sunlight, and our cavalcade was advancing up the shore of a June-blue, gorgeous lake. What a morning! The jungle growth shouldering up the lake bank peacock-colored, perfumed, exhaling early mists. Somewhere water spilling down a tiny gorge. Africa at her best.

Great water birds—herons, spur-winged geese, fish eagles, marabou—took flight at our approach; our black boys chattered and sang as they padded along, stork-legged and grotesque with bundles balanced on their woolly knobs; my companion collectors expressed fine fettle.

"Tanganyika!" The Belgian naturalist waved a hand. "Finest of inland lakes. *Sacré!* What bird life!"

Peter Firestone was almost jubilant; sniffing through his short British nose; jaunty in saddle. "Looks jolly good to me. Glad to be here again. I was on these waters in… I say, there's our outpost!"

He pointed. Some half mile up the shore a headland thrust emerald banks into the lake; and we could see the dun-colored walls and tin roof of a blockhouse. Sunshine glittered on the not unfriendly barrel of a small field gun guarding a parade ground before an open gate, and a Union Jack fluttered gayly on its staff.

Firestone cheered. "Fort Kijongo! Look at that flag. Seems dashed good to see that old banner of mine, again. All right, lads. I've got official introductions in my pocket. Let's ride in and see the garrison. I could do with a whisky peg this morning, myself. Pretty quiet, though, isn't it?"

IT WAS. Pretty quiet. Spurring our mounts, we rode down on the little outpost, glad to see a mark of civilization, again. But, instead of a mounted guard to greet us in the outpost gateway, there was nothing save a little whorl of brown dust. The field

within the walls seemed deserted. The blockhouse and atten-
dant buildings were quiet, bathed in hot sunshine. The place was
soundless. Uncertain, we drew up in saddle.

"Must all be at mess," Firestone guessed. "There's only a handful here, anyway. Two squads of Tommies, as I recall. I've been
here before. Stand by, while I run in and look up the commandant."

A moment later, and the Englishman was back in the gateway. For a moment he stood staring at us, one hand brushing
at a lock of sandy hair that troubled his eyes, his face a study, in
the early daylight.

"I say!" He seemed to have trouble working his tongue. "Come
in and have a look. There's something blooming strange."

We were off our horses in half a minute; following Firestone
across the empty parade field. Into an empty barracks house.
Through an empty guard room. Into an empty canteen and into
a mess hall where no man sat at table. This was not right, for the
table was ready. There were coffee cups half full. Plates in which
cold food lay heaped ranged the board. Platters of cut bread. But
no single, solitary man sat to wield the outlaid cutlery. Sunlight
slanting through the windows found a room abandoned to warm
shadows. A faint, insistent buzzing disturbed the piling quiet.
Flies, alone, enjoyed the feast.

The six of us, de Lanrezac, Carpetsi, Garonne, Filipich, old
von Letterbeck and I, just stared. Our English companion
mopped pallid cheeks. His voice was low.

"That looks like last night's dinner. Just served. And listen!
There's not a soul in this outpost. The guns are all stacked along
the wall and there's a fire still smoldering in the cookhouse. But
there's not one blasted soldier in the place."

I tell you it was something to make you look nervously over
your shoulder; something to dampen your palms. A garrison
of men don't sit down to a meal, abandon it after the first three
bites, and vanish hand and foot and body from the outpost.
Unless there are ghosts to whisk them away, or—Tracks! Feofan

Filipich, the Russian elephant hunter, dashed about the little fortress and came back nonplused.

"There are tracks, my friends! But the land beyond the post is swampy. Impossible to tell whether ten or a hundred men have marched around. And when the tracks were made I cannot say. By the saints!"

"*Sapristi!*" Gustav Garonne gestured in excitement. "I have searched the quarters of the men. Everything is in perfect order."

De Lanrezac and Firestone and I raced through the headquarters house. There were army orders on an ant-eaten desk; cots prepared for the night, mosquito netting ready; a pair of polished cavalry boots standing on a camp table; a bottle of Old Crusted, half full. A carbide lamp on the desk was burning weakly; a tunic wearing captain's insignia hung neatly on the back of a chair. Firestone tore through the sheaf of papers.

"Post in command of Captain Charles J. Hilton, K.A.R. Met him somewhere on the coast a long time ago. Good chap. Sandhurst man. His papers are in perfect order. Nothing to indicate trouble." Firestone's face was moist. So was mine. De Lanrezac swore.

"Never have I seen such a thing. I have heard of ships abandoned so. But never an outpost in such desertion."

It was after Firestone had rushed through the headquarters reports, the rest of us had darted about the uncanny place looking for and finding no hint of things amiss to call a garrison from dinner, that I came on the old German, von Letterbeck, standing aloof on the point of the headland, staring, silent in thought, eyes fixed immobile on the blue horizon of Tanganyika. Of the crowd of us, the German alone was calm. Standing and watching the clement lake. Immutable in his steel of reserve. As if nothing untoward had happened, hands quiet on his folded arms. And I, naked-nerved, in the presence of ghosts.

"Von Letterbeck!" I yelled at him. "Don't stand there, man. We've got to do something. De Lanrezac says there's a Belgian outpost fifty miles up the coast from here, and we're going to ride for it…. What do *you* think happened to the men of this British post?"

The old German shrugged. What the devil did he see out there on the horizon? He turned, and there was a frown between the eyes of his creased, stern face.

"Who knows? Perhaps they were called to a fight."

"But their guns are stacked along the wall!"

He nodded. "It is mysterious. But this is mysterious country, *mein freund.* A hard, splendid land—eh! *Ach,* you wish to hurry to the Belgian outpost, then! Perhaps that is the thing to do. We had better report this trouble. I am with you."

WE DID not tell our black *safari.* Your African native is the most superstitious creature on earth, and those bearers of ours would have bolted like antelopes in the presence of this enigma. Let me tell you, I could have bolted myself. It may not sound scary in the telling, but it was scary in the seeing—that African-deep outpost with its abandoned dining table and emptied quarters without a trace to tell why.

So we left the *safari* in charge of the head bearer, a Mang-Battu boy who went by the name of Alfred, wore a straw hat and was shrewd as he was trustworthy. De Lanrezac instructed the black giant to follow us up the coast, explaining something of the emergency; and the African's face showed fear.

"Witchcraft!" he gasped out in his thick dialect. "Spirits! There has been no trouble with the tribesmen, for those I met on the trail this way have spoken words of peace, and the drums at night have talked friendship with you and your kind. The Evil One has carried the men of the fort away. The Evil One dwells on this coast. You pass through the country of demons!"

But we knew he would lead the *safari* after us, for we were protection, payment and food; and we started on a gallop for the Belgian post on the Urindi border. Never have I seen such jungle. Our trail, curving along the rim of the lake, led through swamp and thicket into dripping, dank vegetal forests black as midnight. We had hoped to pick up the track of the vanished soldiers—surely they had marched off somewhere. But the two elephant hunters could find no trail in the swamp bottoms, and the only thing to do was get in touch with the Belgian garrison. There was a telegraph at the Belgian post, de Lanrezac explained, and we could spread an alarm.

I think all of us were apprehensive of the same thing; believed the soldiers had been surprised and swept off by rebellious tribesmen. But of savages the jungle gave no sign. We might have been the first to ride through there since the day those jungles sprouted from the primal muck. The silence, a stifling blanket in the perfumed heat, was enervating. Each twist in the difficult path gave promise of poisoned darts fired from ambush, and if ever I saw shadows where goblins could hide I saw them spread deep in that viny morass.

Late afternoon, with the sun growing dim and the shadows thick. Tanganyika Lake was roughening; we could hear the somber wash of tumbling surf and occasionally, through a rift in the trees, catch a glimpse of white-capped water. Single file we rode; elephant guns slung ready to hand, nerves taut for the unexpected. Certainly the unexpected lurked somewhere in that dank jungly shore. What evil had overtaken the men in that British post? The question hammered again and again through my mind. Those soldiers had listened to mess call, filed to the mess room, sat ready to grab forks and spoons.

"Must have been just about the time we were yarning around the fire," Peter Firestone had declared. "They mess late." Then something had interrupted that meal; yanked them magically away....

CHAPTER III

OUT OF THE PAST

STRANGE HOW OLD von Letterbeck had taken the lead. I wondered if the others had noticed. Now the old German was riding at our head, square-shouldered, ramrod-stiff as ever in his saddle, unperturbed.

"The path is bad that way," he said once when we came to a fork in the trail. "Let us follow the beach." Again: "That will be a muddy road. Bogs. This way is better. We ford a shallow stream."

His face was chiseled from stone, shadowed by the brim of his sun helmet. His eyes without emotion. But he seemed to know the way.

"You're right," Firestone or de Lanrezac or Filipich would agree. "I remember, too." But the strange thing was, how did von Letterbeck know? Perhaps, long ago, he had hunted this shore. We were all too excited to wonder on this. Besides, one did not ask von Letterbeck questions. We followed his advices and found them accurate.

The sun westered early. Thunderheads billowed down the far horizon of the lake, and twilight brought a brief, pounding shower that made of the trail a quagmire. The rain stopped as quickly as its start, but our drenched horses floundered in mud, and a night lighted thinly by timid stars stopped our race.

"We are but six miles from the Belgian post," de Lanrezac decided. "But we must make camp and wait till dawn. It would be too bad to lose the way in this night."

We found an upland, built a raging fire, and spread blankets. We would sleep with rifles under our hands.

"I think," said von Letterbeck, moving in the firelight, "I will have my evening ride. To reconnoiter a bit. If blacks lurk nearby I will spread an alarm. A precaution."

The Russian elephant hunter and the French collector voiced a protest; but von Letterbeck, unhearing, had gone. A long time later I woke to see him, shadowy in the gloom, arranging his blankets. Then, for a time, he sat staring at the embers of the fire. Finally he unbuckled his automatic, examined the cartridge clip, slipped it back into the holster. His glance strayed to the men snoring in their blankets near him; then, with a twist of his military mustache, he lay back on the ground and snored with them.

Garonne's hand, patting my arm, woke me. The sun was scarcely up. Pale mists writhed from the grass and the dew was chill. My companions were unleashing their hobbled mounts. We lost no time over morning coffee; again our little column filed along the trail. The sun rose with a blast of heat and the jungle steamed. Our road improved; soon we were spurring at a fast gallop.

"It is not far," von Letterbeck observed. "Beyond that hill."

De Lanrezac, in the lead, pointed out a clearing. A thorny fence reared in a compound cut from a sandalwood grove. The dun-hued blockhouse with its tin roof and gun-guarded gate was almost identical with that of the British post we had left. We could see a drill field and a headquarters house over which waved the black, yellow and red of Belgium.

But the point of similarity did not stop there. Would to God it had! For we rode through a gate where no guard stood. De Lanrezac flung from his saddle to sprint into the headquarters hut and return with a shout on his lips. When we clamored through a vacant barracks room and entered a mess hall, not a man of us could utter a sound. The same sunshine dropping through open windows. The same table, set with plates of untouched food, filled flagons, unemptied wine decanters. The same flies buzzing over an abandoned dinner.

There were the guns in their precise stacks, the kits of the men in order, the house of the commandant undisturbed.

"Mother of us all!" de Lanrezac screeched at last. Sweat beads were traveling down his leathern cheeks. "There should be a

squad of Askaris here. Two white lieutenants and the commandant. And there is no man!"

Not a soldier occupied the post. Only tomb-like silence and
the gold-heavy African sunshine.

BELIEVE ME, when we went over every inch of that fort,
found footprints leading into a water swamp behind the hill,
lost the tracks, returned to the blockhouse and discovered the
telegraph instruments smashed to junk—then there was something doing. No hoodoo ghost had wrecked that telegraph, and
we walked with automatics in our hands.

"No telling who did it!" Firestone raved, flinging a fist at the
ambient jungle that simmered about the thorn fence. "But we've
got to get help. Listen! We'll hit for Uzumbura. It's a British
base. Long run, but we can put up to-night at a place I know
along the lake. Used to be a naval post a few years back. Nobody
there now, but it's a good place to camp. There's a firing wall
and an empty blockhouse. We'll stay there to-night and get to
Uzumbura to-morrow. If this is an uprising...."

Well, if it was an uprising we'd give a strong account of
ourselves in a scrap. Riding bunched together, we hit the trail
at a fast gallop, alert as tigers for every sound or moving shadow.
I won't forget the ride we made that day up the north border of
Tanganyika Lake. Jungle? It closed in behind us like a clutching
green hand and shut down over our heads like a smothering lid.
Steamy, sour, and hot. And twice as quiet as the soundless world
where the Bantus say the were-folk keep their haunts.

My companions spoke little, and then to swear. If they were
like me, the sight of that second magic-emptied mess hall had
given their nerves a mighty savage wrench. Filipich, the tall
Russian, kept sponging sweat from his face. Garonne jabbed a
flask into his beard at every halt. The Italian, Carpetsi, darted
glances back over his shoulder.

An African jungle is spooky enough at best; this hinterland
was alive with an unknown danger that brewed among the black

trees. All of us were like a lot of tight-strung wires. I'm wrong. All, that is, save old Hilmar von Letterbeck.

If the German had nerves he did not show them. His only comment on the abandoned Belgian post had been a gruff: *"Herr Gott!"* Now he rode along, oblivious. Occasionally he would growl to himself. "An easy trail to follow, this." A twist at his fierce mustache. "We can reach Herr Firestone's suggested camp in easy time."

We reached Girombo at sunset. All afternoon we had caught no view of the lake. Now our path plunged suddenly from dense undergrowth. We saw a shoulder of barren, steep hill rearing from the rim of the lake, at its crest a shabby blockhouse surrounded by the usual thorny *zareeba* and fence of pointed stakes, head-high.

The unfrequented outpost overlooked a shallow bay in which rotted the remains of a pier. The position of the blockhouse was admirable. To approach, the enemy must climb that slope, the only cover being low clumps of brier. The blockhouse we found dropping with foul decay, but the surrounding stake wall was in fine repair. Hobbling our horses in the blockhouse, we dumped our kits behind the wall; prepared to sleep in the open.

I was mighty glad to be sleeping behind that protection. The jungle about us was too desolate and still; the lake below was so calm as to be unreal. The dank air, too, was motionless, *as* if the very atmosphere were sneakily gathering itself together for a crash. The smoke from our camp fire drifted straight upward into the darkening sky.

HUNGRY AS we were, we ate with difficulty. Food and nerves don't work well together. To my surprise, I noticed that von Letterbeck ate least of all. Outwardly he was still unmoved as rock, silent, his saturnine face almost expressionless in the hard etching of firelight. His unwinking eyes fixed on the fire. Eyes like unseeing metal. His only gesture to tweak that bristling mustache. A von Hindenburg watching the fortunes of war might have worn the same implacable face.

But the others were under tension; burst into a sudden chatter of speculations and conjectures. Firestone was chafing.

"This blasted vanishing of two garrisons has my head ajangle," he complained. "What the deuce can it mean? If it was a native uprising their drums would be going like mad, and instead, it's silent as hell. I say, we'd better post a guard to-night. Just in case. Won't need to worry, though. If anything attacked us we could hold out beautifully. Y'know, I once struck it something like this, and on this very spot. It was during the war. Right here. I was the only man in this blooming outpost, too."

De Lanrezac exclaimed in surprise. "You were here during the war?"

"Just about four years ago, back in 1916," the Englishman explained. "Maybe you heard of the fighting on this lake. Say, it's an old battleground of mine. No end of scrapping, too. The Belgians owned all the west shore of the lake and the Germans ruled the east bank. The Germans had put some mighty tough gunboats on the water. The Kingani and Graf von Gotson and some others. Had a big army too. To oust 'em, the British organized a Naval Africa Expedition. I was a lieutenant in the outfit. We trekked a couple of gunboats, Mimi and the Tou-Tou, all the way across Belgian Congo and dropped 'em in the lake. Real naval war we staged. Captured the Kingani after a ruddy go and finally sank a new German boat, the von Wissman."

Young Firestone's face glowed with enthusiasm. "Biggest adventure of the war, that naval fight on this lake. And this place, Girombo, was a base. We had a lot of guns hidden in this blockhouse, and one night I ran a launch into this bay. I was the only man on that launch, too. All by myself I ran her up the Belgian coast and over here to pick up a crew and load the cargo of guns. But I got there, and there wasn't a soul around. The reïnforcements I'd expected had been waylaid somewhere and there wasn't a man to help me.

"For three days I stuck in this hole, loading those machine guns. Maybe you think I wasn't in a beastly funk, too. Easi-

est thing in the world for the German commandant down at
their base fifty miles away to know I was in the place. All he'd
have had to do was send a party down on my neck. They'd have
captured me and that launch and those guns. They'd have found
information that might have helped 'em to win back the whole
lake.

"Why, the whole fate of their African campaign lay in my
launch. For I had maps and munitions of utmost importance,
and those guns were, later, to outfit a Belgian corps that finally
swept Germany out of this territory. And there I was, alone,
stowing the whole business!"

Firestone laughed, and went on: "Can you fancy how one lone
German soldier could have charged me while I was loading that
cargo with my back turned? But the Germans never showed up.
At last my men arrived. We rushed the launch away. Outfitted
the Belgians and finally blew the Germans clean off Tanganyika. I always wondered about my unholy good luck—why that
German commander never sent men to capture this outpost."

AND THEN the extraordinary occurred. We'd been ranged in
a circle about the fire, listening to the Englishman, glad of the
unexpected yarn and relief of former tension. Now the circle
was rudely broken.

"But I did send a man!" The words crackled sharp above the
snap of blazing timbers. And there was old von Letterbeck, stiff
on his feet, hands clenched to fists, veins bulging like red threads
on his forehead, eyes like nail heads agleam.

"Gott im Himmel!" he blazed at Firestone. "Did you British
think the German command was such a fool?

"But maybe I was. For I sent what I thought was the best man
I had. I knew one soldier of Germany could take this outpost,
and my men were few and I could spare but one. I picked what
I thought my best man, a lieutenant, strong as an ox, formerly
brave.

" 'Go to-night and capture that outpost!' I told him. 'The fate
of Germany in Africa may depend on you. How you take the

post I care not, but win it you must, and alone. All of Germany will trust you on this mission. Fail to capture that outpost and your Fatherland will never wish to see your face again!'

"That weakling soldier! 'I will capture it!' he promised." Von Letterbeck smashed fist against palm. "Bah! This man I trusted beyond words. He failed. He did not take your post. Never was he heard of again. You ran your guns safely. You beat us. We lost East Africa. Perhaps we lost the whole war. 'Take that outpost if it is the last thing you ever live to do!' was my command. He—did not—obey!"

A stream of sweat wriggled down von Letterbeck's cheek. An oath burst from his teeth. Wheeling sharply, he strode from the firelight, stamped through the gate of the *zareeba* and marched off down the hill; plunged alone into the dusk of the thicket.

For a long time none of us could speak. At last it was little Garonne. *"Quel dommage!* A pity. No wonder he has hated this trek! I did not think to remember that this territory once belonged to them. So he was in command—and lost. That is how he knows so well the trail."

Firestone's voice was grave. "How beastly sorry I am! Did you see his face? Stricken. Those soldiers of the old school! His Fatherland—thinks he's failed it. I never thought about him listening to me recite that rubbish. Seems so dashed long ago, and all. Much less that *he*—"

"Hate to see him wander off on another of his evening excursions," I said, strolling nervously to the picket fence. I hadn't forgotten the emergency, by any means, in spite of the shock dealt us by the old German.

I could appreciate his feelings, too. It would be anguish to travel a lost country, and remember the old days. The old fire-eating warrior would never forget his defeat. I stared at the lake. The shore was washed with peaceful water and a violet haze softened the jungle. Where lake met sky the last faint tint of sunset faded and beyond a distant purple headland the moon, a giant wheel of crimson, drifted gently through a thin green feather of cloud. I turned back toward the fire.

Crash! An explosion smashed a red hole through the hazy underbrush screening the foot of the slope. *Smash! Smash! Smash!* My sun helmet spun, riddled, from my head. A rain of bullets screamed past my ear, and all Hades let loose with a roar.

CHAPTER IV

JUNGLE SIEGE

"FIGHT!" SCREECHED FIRESTONE. Yelling, the others about the fire snatched up their rifles and sprang to the wall. Carpetsi dashed into the blockhouse to get our elephant guns, and Garonne raced to our dunnage heap for cartridge belts.

Stunned, I stooped to pick up my bullet-drilled helmet; then flung back on the thorn fence, my Kirby spouting flame. I wonder if you can see the picture, then? The six of us hanging on that barricade, rifles whanging a steady roar, gun-flame stabbing the gloom, powder-smoke adrift and pungent in the tepid air.

There was Filipich, the Russian, wild hair blowing, a grin in his teeth, yells and strange Slavic oaths streaming from his beard. De Lanrezac, dancing and dodging from one stake to another, pumping his automatic, his face dripping. Garonne, kneeling on one side of me, rifle barrel thrust through a niche in the fence, his finger fleet on trigger. Carpetsi, sharp-shooting on the other side, hands flying from cartridge belt to gun, teeth a-gleam, lusty Roman curses on his lips. And last in line, Firestone; his British face livid, his gun going like a machine.

How we sprayed the underbrush down that slope! One, two, three we shot! Tossed down smoking automatics for Kirbys. Flung aside the Kirbys for those .475 elephant guns. Halted to load all three and start again. The din clamored off across the dark lake. The smoke bulged high in the moonlight. We poured a river of scalding lead down that barren hill, and the enemy, unseen at the bottom, returned the fire with interest. Triple interest. *R'rrrrrrt!* came the roar; and a scythe of bullets swept our barricade.

"A machine gun!" Firestone yelled.

"A Chaut-Chaut automatic," screamed de Lanrezac. "They must have taken it from the Belgian post. *Mon Dieu!*" His oath came shrill, for the rapid-fire gun had stopped, a rifle had snapped, *spang!* And the little Belgian waved in the air a blood-streaked hand. "Sharpshooter! Got me through the fist. Broke my fingers!"

I emptied my elephant gun at the bush clump whence that deadly accurate shot had come. But my fire was answered by no stricken wail; and the machine gun's roar burst anew from behind a pale bowlder deep in the underbrush. The bullets ripped up the slope and knifed through our thorny-stake fence.

Hunched low to avoid the flailing fusillade, we poured a storm of shot at that bowlder. Chips flew from the stone like sparks; the rapid-fire gun stopped; a moment later came a torrid blaze of rifle shot from a bush in another quarter. We directed our fire at the bush and it was answered by a salvo from a nest of trees on the opposite side of the bowlder.

"Must be fifty men down there!" Firestone cursed fiercely. "And I can't locate one. Every minute the shots come from another spot!"

IT WAS uncanny. If there was a mob in that underbrush we should certainly have hit something. We poured a leaden rain at the point where enemy flame blazed; only to be answered from a different angle. Gunfire burst here and there from the hazy brush, would halt, and the machine gun would let go. That machine gun was murderous, but the rifle fire was sheer magic. There were marksmen down there with eyes like hawks. More than one bullet whined through my hair the second my unwary head reared an inch above our fence.

"Shoot with care!" Filipich bawled. "Saint Mitrophane! We are fighting master snipers. There are but five of us now, and—"

Spang! It was Garonne who got it. The Frenchman rocked back on his heels with a yell, clutching a crimson shoulder.

"The arm is broken. *Mère de Dieu!*" Yes! Sharpshooting, indeed. That bullet had spun through a three-inch hole in the fence and picked off the Frenchman's gun arm.

And we had gained no view of an enemy—only those flowering bursts of gunfire spurting out of the undergrowth. The sweat sprouted out on my cheeks. The machine gun chattered and the air overhead droned. "Keep heads down!" The leaden hail spattered against the blockhouse behind us. "Lookout!"

But Filipich was too late. He had thrust his Kirby over the rim of the fence in an attempt to level a bead on that bowlder. No sooner had his arm been exposed than a rifle had cracked in the bush. The tall Russian roared. The Kirby clattered from his fists and he was dancing backward with a shattered elbow.

I tell you, the air was purple then. There were Garonne, Filipich and de Lanrezac out of commission, winged as cutely as if the devil himself had done the shooting; and two seconds later Carpetsi, the Italian, got a machine gun slug across the forehead and spilled to his face unconscious as a felled tree. I glared at Peter Firestone, and the Englishman's face was twisting.

"They've fired only once to every six of our shots," he gasped. "We'll be shot to shreds at this rate. Don't shoot till you see a face. Wait."

De Lanrezac and Garonne stumbled over to the Italian and made shift to drag his body to cover. Filipich was fumbling with his useless arm. Firestone and I knelt, gasping, behind the wall where it was thickest, and waited. We didn't have to wait a split minute-tick, either. The minute our fire ceased, a wild, strange, unbelievable sound burst from that undergrowth at slope's bottom. A sound to make us think we were mad. The shrill, blood-stirring blast of a bugle!

A bugle! Bell-clear, the blatant horn-note blared out into the stunned night and echoed away and away across the waters of Tanganyika Lake. And no sooner than the preposterous fanfare had died away, a specter ten thousand times as incredible took shape at the foot of that hill below. Firestone's eyes were starting from his head, his lips gurgling. De Lanrezac, Filipich and Garonne crawled forward to look, and were turned to stone. As for me, my head might have been trepanned. Remember, this was an African jungle, the shore of Tanganyika, deep wilderness. Africa!

THERE AT the foot of the hill below our barricade, conjured by the notes of a banshee trumpet, ghostly in the wraith-light of the low-cruising moon, stood a soldier of the German army, straight from the vanished past. In his hands a heavy Mauser rifle. His body clad in the shreds of regulation gray-green; belt and trappings a-gleam, army boots rotted to mere blobs of leather, but polished to shine like coal.

The iron, spiked officer's helmet with its polished visor and imperial eagle on the crest was a thing unreal as a dream, but the face below it was sheerest phantasy, so worn and thin and eaten as to appear a mere shrunken skull. I tell you, the thing was goblin. Yet, the eyes in that witch-face burned like fox fires. The frail hands moved to lift the Mauser rifle. And slowly the apparition started its march up the hill.

Out of the underbrush and up the hill it came, propelled, surely, by magic. God knows how we lifted our guns, Firestone and I. But I found myself watching it through the sights of my elephant rifle; and I heard my companion's gun roar. My own weapon jumped and spat flame. But the vision never stopped; I swear it began to *run!*

The Mauser flashed and the bullets whipped close past my head. *Crack!* I heard my gun go. The thing flickering through the sights seemed to halt for a pace; then on it came, rifle hammering. On up the hill. Straight up to our fence of thorn. And terrible as nightmare, with blood leaking from its goblin mouth and flame squirting from that gun.

He might have got us, too, for I swear he reached the gate. No bullet from an Allied gun could have stopped that German soldier. No! You may think in our raw-nerved astonishment we missed our mark. But I swear he was shot to sponge halfway up, and charged on. Reached the gate, I say, with gun hammering.

Then came a shot from the jungle behind him. *Wham!* And there, down the slope, knelt von Letterbeck, a smoking automatic in his fist. The soldier tangled on the fence of thorns stared quietly at the moon.

"HEARD THE shooting," the old German collector panted at us, "and started to run." He limped painfully forward. "Tripped. Caught my ankle in a trap of roots. Fractured a small bone, I guess. But I got here to find that undergrowth down there planted with guns. Some of them had strings tied to trigger. There's a Belgian Chaut-Chaut, too. Then I saw this bandit—*Herr Gott!*"

I had scarcely heard old von Letterbeck's words. I had been thinking of that lone, thin wraith dashing from gun to gun, pulling strings, springing to fire the Chaut-Chaut, darting to snipe a shot or two—*one* man staging that assault. But von Letterbeck's oath exploded something in my head; gave the first, mad inkling.

The soldier lay by the fire. Riddled by our .475s, even with von Letterbeck's shot in his spine, he was not for dying. Silent he lay, his frail, crimson-splashed frame on a mat of blood, staring. But the fire glow found the eyes alive in the face so incredible beneath that incredible helmet. What the eyes saw no man could say, but when von Letterbeck swore those eyes glowed to smile.

The old German collector had hobbled forward, dropped on his knees. The voice was like dry wind, like a husk. *"Lieutenant—*it is *you!* Lieutenant—Gulick—"

The rest of us were silent, I can promise you. Even Carpetsi, come conscious with his wounded head and wobbling on his feet, was quiet. So we could hear the words that seemed to come like echoes from gone yesterday.

"Ja, it is I, Herr Colonel. You are here—with the Germans. I

see—them standing around you. Then—then the British are—gone? I—I am not too late. I had feared. For when I started—the savages—captured me. Carried me far away. So far! A lost jungle. Held me—prisoner for days. How many? I cannot recall. But I escaped. Wandered back. It—seemed like—many years."

The fire snapped and sputtered. Von Letterbeck's face was gray, gemmed with sweat.

The echo went on: "Like years…. But I never—gave up. On, on I wandered. Then I came—to—British outpost. Charged. Men at mess. Captured them—without fight." (And no wonder!) "Drove them into swamp—where—could not find way out. Then on—to another post—Belgian Askaris. Captured them, *ja*. The same. So many enemies—in our territory. But I found—this post. Knew must charge. Fixed guns—look like many men. Cavalry bugle…. Then I was not too late! Then I—we are winning. Germany will win—the war. The Fatherland—will be proud. Have won—"

I wept. Shamelessly. I heard Firestone's shaky whisper: "Four years! Think of it! Lost! Forgetting time! Only remembering his country." And de Lanrezac's groan: "What a soldier!"

Only old von Letterbeck did not weep. *"Ja,"* he said softly. "The Fatherland will be proud. We—you have won." Softly. *"Ja,* Gulick—won."

The fading eyes beneath the crested helmet smiled. "The soldiers with you," came the whisper. "I should like—again to hear it. Could they sing—sing for me—'Die Wacht am Rhein' for me—to hear?"

I tell you, I was always glad afterward for the sour hours I'd put in learning a naturalist's quota of German. Von Letterbeck turned his face to us, and we understood. Can you see us there? Can you see us standing about that ghostly, vanishing soldier in gray-green with his pitiful helmet and gray, fantastic face? The fire snapping gently. The jungle behind the blockhouse whispering. The round moon high and silvery above that African lake.

Yes, we sang! De Lanrezac, the Belgian, clutching his smashed fingers. Filipich, the Russian, holding tight a broken elbow. Garonne, the Frenchman, with his bloodied arm. Carpetsi of Italy, a scarlet rag about his dark head. Firestone of England. And a Yankee. Lord, do you get it? The drama of it? Old von Letterbeck stood like a ramrod to lead in the stirring song; and the pain in our faces came not from our wounds, as we sang. The Watch on The Rhine!

> *"A peal like thunder*
> *Calls the brave…."*

But it was not until we made our slow march from the outpost to the thicket on the shore, where waited the new-dug grave, that I knew. I was wrapping him in von Letterbeck's greatcoat, and I saw the little tag that soldiers wear in the breast of the tunic. A little metal identification tag. The name: GULICK VON LETTERBECK.

BRADSHAW, THE Kelantan naturalist, gained his feet with a sigh, and rapped cold ashes from his pipe. "We dropped back to Kijongo," he resumed with a growl. "Found the Tommies. They'd gotten themselves out of the trackless swamp where he'd marched them, and they were a sheepish lot. Same at the Belgian post. They were all right. But think of it! Think of that lonely young soldier holding up those garrisons, braving that last charge, arranging that assault—after four time-lost years trapped in African jungle. One *would* forget time in that wilderness. Lose the years. And he—Think of it! Never knowing the war was over, and—"

The naturalist's voice choked out. The crickets chirped in the quiet, and moonlight spangled the bay beyond the veranda. Bradshaw turned on us a sudden smile.

"But I wish you could have seen his old man. Old von Letterbeck, I mean. On the trail from there. The best of good fellows. Gay at camp fire. Talked and chuckled and yarned and chattered all the way back to the coast."

YANKEE BEWARE!

Peter Scarlet battles a threefold doom on the wild, crag-littered coast of Turkestan.... Behind him a Russian bloodhound leads a scavenger pack. Before him spreads the blazing lake—and death for the unbeliever

The Ghost Khan sits in a lake of fire
Green emeralds in his crown
Let the foes of Allah all beware
Let unbelievers learn faith there
Nor touch the gems in the Ghost Khan's Hair
Lest the Ghost Khan laugh them down.

—Rune of the Green-eyed Medjidie.

SOMETHING WAS DOING up on the bridge. The skipper's crass voice had been bellowing all afternoon to accompany the sound of smashing vodka bottles. Already three sailors had stumbled for the fo'c'sle with hands pressed to bleeding mouths or swollen ears.

And the deck passengers crammed amidships were something else again. Those fifty Moslem pilgrims bound for some Turkestan shrine hadn't taken their eyes off the bridge all day, a crowd of hooded ghosts, quiet as so many mice. But a Yankee who knows his East wouldn't be fooled. A quiet Moslem may be only planning the place where his dagger shall stab.

On the bridge the drunken skipper in his cabin was roaring. On the deck below sat the well behaved specters, waiting.

Peter Scarlet, the little American curio hunter, didn't like the looks of things. Standing at the starboard rail under the bridge he watched the passing coast with a mounting sense of apprehension. In the twilight the coast was an unreality. Desolate was

the word. The mountains made a fence of shadows rimming
the unknown. Maybe Turkestan lay behind them and maybe it
didn't. The beach was rocky, naked, ashen. Driftwood piled the
shore like mounds of old bones.

The Caspian Sea was a rolling expanse of dank bilge, sweeping south to where Persia lay. "Swill water," the old Moslem
bumboat man at Abassabad had called it. "Thrown there from
Allah's washtubs to poison the country. The coast is dead, *hazoor*.
A place of jackals and skulls. Not a healthy place."

It was no place to cruise on a rotten coastal steamer that
might explode with trouble any minute and send its only American passenger shoreward with a knife in his neck-nape. Peter
Scarlet's hand stole nervously to his Luger-weighted hip. It
needed no little dicky bird to tell the curio hunter that trouble
was on the way. *The Little Flower of Mercy* was a Russian tramp
to begin with, a vagabond, rotten from bow to stern, scarred by
every port in the East. If her fo'c'sle was a slum filled with human
garbage, her skipper was the A-1 garbage man. The moment
he had swung up *The Little Flower of Mercy's* gangway and seen
her big Russian skipper, Peter Scarlet had thanked God for the
Luger on his belt.

The little American curio hunter had cut his sign on most
of the Asian out-trails; seen some mighty tough exhibits on
the route. But none to match the skipper of *The Little Flower*

of Mercy. Seven feet off the deck he towered on his bare sea-heels. His name was Rachmaninoff. A stomach like a barrel, arms thick as masts. His shoulders were tattooed slabs of beef and his chest was like the prow of a bulldog schooner weedy with a mat of hair. The head on top was a spoiled muskmelon, grotesquely too small for the body, bald as a post with a queer pinkish scar scribbled in an arc across the skull. A black, Jehovan beard bushed wildly from the jaw. The eyes were rancid yellow dots to port and starboard of the battered nose. The owner of this false-face had achieved extraordinary evil by clamping pince-nez glasses in its middle, a fine gold chain attaching them to one ear. Pince-nez glasses and three pistols in his belt. That was Rachmaninoff, the skipper. When Rachmaninoff roared a few more pedals dropped off *The Little Flower of Mercy;* the crew of garbage shivered.

LET A steamer's skipper bawl bombast at his crew, but let him speak with softness to a Moslem holy man leading fifty Turkoman pilgrims. Peter Scarlet could see the old priest squatting in the middle of his crowd of ghosts, and from the looks of things Scarlet guessed he was no ordinary hadji and nobody's fool. A mummy wrapped in a snowy robe, he was, with the green turban of one who had kissed Mohammed's Kaba-stone and sipped the waters of Zem. On his bosom he wore the Order of Medjidie; there was pride in his shrunken leather face. It was his eyes that lifted him too far above the ordinary and his voice that kept him there. That was a wizard's voice, and the eyes had come straight out of a Persian cat, green and luminous in dusk.

Rachmaninoff, the Russian skipper, was not a subtle soul. When the priest and his fifty followers had boarded *The Little Flower of Mercy* that morning, the good Captain Rachmaninoff had scorched them with torrid profanity for not clearing the gangway quicker. He had even dropped a hairy paw on the holy man's arm to speed him along the deck. The priest had said nothing and the pilgrims had said nothing. But all day long they had studied the bridge. The silence had seemed to sweat.

Peter Scarlet had sweated, too. Now he listened to the rumpus on the bridge and he watched the pilgrims huddled on the heaving deck and he kept his hand mighty close to the Luger automatic. That German pistol was Scarlet's best friend, and his only friend just now. In all his days he had never known it to miss. He caressed its polished butt with a thumb and waited.

The Little Flower of Mercy bucked a head sea red with sunset. Hot words drifted down from above. The priest with the green eyes had started a few words of his own. His brown hands were waving an abacadabra at the ghosts crowded about him and his voice drifted weird down the breeze. That old wizard was spinning his boys a yarn to keep them quiet, Scarlet guessed. But suddenly the little curio hunter pricked up his ears.

"And on yonder shore," droned the ancient one's echo, "on yonder shore, my sons, the mighty Jenghiz came. It was there, by Allah, he left his ghost to rest. There in a lake of fire stayed his ghost with the emerald crown. And when the moon of Allah is full, my sons, and the One God sees fit to call, then the ghost of the dead Khan rises from the lake and talks with the One God again.

"I have seen," droned the chant. "I have seen. By the will of Allah (on whom be the blessing), I have seen the ghost of the Khan. The emerald crown is like the glory of the East and the ghost of Jenghiz laughs to tell Allah the compassionate how that glory will shine once again. For Allah is great and merciful and the Believer may see the crown and hear the magic laugh where the Unbeliever must die." The echoed sighed, and a brown hand waved. "It was on yonder shore where I saw and heard the mighty Jenghiz and his laughter...."

Those fifty pilgrims weren't listening. They had heard the legend a thousand times, and they were too busy thinking about the Russian giant on the bridge. But Peter Scarlet, the little American curio hunter, listened. He had heard the story of Jenghiz Khan's ghost before and he listened every time. That ghost rose out of a boiling Turkestan lake, and it laughed out loud in the moonlight. There were emeralds on the apparition's brow that rivaled the size of the stars. But only the beloved of Allah, said the legend, could look on the ghost and hear its laugh and live. For the ghost's laugh slew the unfaithful, and they never came back to tell.

The funny part of it was they never *had* come back, those unfaithful. Peter Scarlet remembered seven men who had gone out to hunt that emerald crown and had never somehow returned. Any reader of history knew how Jenghiz Khan had wandered up a Turkestan valley one evening sporting the famous emerald crown, and returned to his legionnaires minus the treasure.

No one knew just where the valley was and the crown had never been found. But the Moslems had built the great legend, and a sweat damped Scarlet's forehead as he stood there on the deck of *The Little Flower of Mercy* and heard this unexpected Medjidie tell his pilgrims he had seen the emeralds and heard the laugh.

"And because I was a True Believer," intoned the chant, "I heard and saw."

To starboard lay the Turkestan coast and ten feet distant sat that priest with the pale green eyes. A bead of sweat coasted down Peter Scarlet's nose as he edged along the rail to get nearer that story teller's voice.

But westward the sun was sinking in a tumble of flaming clouds, the Caspian Sea took fire and the old priest finished with the tale. For the time had come to pray. Bowing up in his snowy mantle, he flung his skinny arms at Mecca and intoned the Islamic chant. The pilgrims faced about for the first time that day and bowed in a rythmic huddle. *"Ash hadu illa il Allah...."*

The prayer was loud, but it didn't drown the scream that spiralled up from the bridge.

SCARLET JUMPED, tight-nerved, saw a sailor in rags come headlong down the bridge ladder and go racing aft up the scuppers. A thread of blood trickled from the seaman's lips. His eyes were scary with fright. A voice bawled like thunder, and

Captain Rachmaninoff's bulk came charging down the ladder
like a rhino in pursuit.

Rachmaninoff's eyes were not kindly behind the dainty
pince-nez on his nose. His sea cap sailed from his scarred skull
as his feet hit the deck with a slam; his Bolshevist whiskers
jutted like metal wire, and he clutched in his fist a vodka bottle
that dripped blood. Down the deck fled the terrified sailor, and
Rachmaninoff went after him with a howl. *"Mohammed an rasool
Al-laah!"* droned the prayerful pilgrims.

The sailor skirted those chanting Moslem passengers like a
breath of wind, but the Russian skipper wasn't skirting anybody.
He wanted to lay that vodka bottle across that sailor's head, and
he cut across the deck and raced into the huddle of Moslems
like a hurricane. Straight into the Moslem prayer meeting
Rachmaninoff charged, and the Followers of the Prophet went
somersaulting like wind-blown bundles of laundry. But the
old Medjidie priest was locked in prayer and never moved. The
Russian ploughed into the huddled old man, tripped, flopped
to his face with a roar.

"Saint Mitrophane!" The giant gained his feet with a scream.
"Trip me, will you? You and your fool mob. Blood of a Cossack,
if I won't punish you to pastry for this—"

Smack! The vodka bottle hit the old priest's shoulder. The
holy man screeched. The bottle exploded like an electric bulb.
The pilgrims let out a tigerish yowl and closed in, but the skipper lashed out two pistols and drove them back. Turning like a
gorilla, he whipped at the holy man with his gun muzzle. Red
mists swirled before Peter Scarlet's eyes. Luger in fist, he sprang
into the mêlée. "Stop" he screamed at the Russian. "Fool! They'll
kill you, you damned rat! Leave the old man alone."

A joyful yowl blew from the giant's beard. Walloping out
with his gun he laid the muzzle across the old priest's jaw. Bone
snapped. Twirling in his cloak, the ancient Medjidie went spinning against the deck rail. Sliding on the slanted deck, Peter
Scarlet skidded to his knees. A terrible wail went up from the

pilgrims. But the old priest was gone over the rail. The Moslems charged in a squalling, whirling tangle. Rachmaninoff's pistol roared, and a sheeted pilgrim crumpled.

SHOUTING OATHS, Scarlet swung his gun. But a blowing cloak slapped across his eyes; next minute a giant hand had trapped his throat. The pilgrims were tumbling like bursting surf, and the big paw yanked Scarlet off the deck.

"I am captain here. You shall learn to defy Rachmaninoff." Grinning teeth gnashed in the curio hunter's face. With one hand the Russian whipped him off his feet, flung him over the turbans of the mob. The deck circled under Scarlet as he sailed through the air; then it rose up and smote him with a whack.

The little American curio hunter hit the scuppers like a sack of grain. His head whaled a wheel-chuck. Japanese lanterns danced before his eyes, but he lurched to his feet with a yell. Peter Scarlet was never as old as his years or the beard on his chin made him look. He got a hand on the deck rail and steadied his Luger, and his eyes turned to little blue beads.

Rachmaninoff was coming for him, plunging through a caterwalling whirlpool of arms and sheets and spinning hoods. Head down, the big Russian charged. Straight at Peter Scarlet that bald skull came like a Roman battering ram. Through the steady gun sights the curio hunter caught a second quick vision—that round skull with its long, pinky scar. It came like a pale cannon ball, and Scarlet's Luger roared. That gun never missed. A spurt of blood founted from the head, but it never stopped traveling. The deck rolled with the charge. The Russian's doubled body hit Peter Scarlet like an express train hits a cat.

Iron rails broke under the impact. The body of the Russian giant and the body of the little American curio hunter hit water with a towering, gelid splash.

CHAPTER II

HIDDEN EMERALDS

"**SWILL WATER,**" **THE** old Moslem bumboat man at Abassabad had called it. "Thrown there from Allah's washtubs to poison the country." Peter Scarlet called it a few other things when he spat the first quart out of his lungs and got his arms to working. That first quart almost sank him and the first wave almost finished him for fair. Lifting him on a lacy crest, the roller flung him under the steamer's stern and he missed the lashing screw by a hair's breadth. It wouldn't be nice to be chopped to hamburg and scattered on the Caspian Sea.

The little American curio hunter wailed and dived. When he gained surface again it was dark. *The Little Flower of Mercy* slid off like a shadowy wall. There was just a spot of lilac reflected on the distant shore. Then the spot of lilac and the shadowy wall dimmed out in a flood of night, and Peter Scarlet knew he was done. But he discovered the Luger still fastened in his clutch; stuck it in his belt. Almost reassuring....

A wave ducked him twice and he doubled in the heaving wash to get at his boots. He felt a little gloomy as the boots left his kicking feet. Somehow he'd always wanted to die with them on. Damn! That Russian's dead head must have cracked a rib or two. A curse slipped out of his sopping beard and he rolled over in the sweeping sea. Pull for the shore, anyhow. The Scarlets would fight Saint Peter at the Golden Gate. But it was a little more jolly to croak in a crowd—

"Damn!" Peter Scarlet swore out loud as he swam. A scream trickled off across the wave and bored like a hot wire through his head. There it was again. Ploughing water with a champion Australian crawl, the little curio hunter tossed caution to the winds and headed for the ghastly sound. The screaming sounded again. That wasn't a human voice. That was the call of lost souls who lay drowned at the bottom of this sea. It must be leaking up from the reasty bottom-mud.

But it wasn't. It whistled up out of a breaking comber ahead; next minute Peter Scarlet was plunging alongside a floating mummy in a robe. A scrawny hand wrapped finger's into his beard and a bobbing head opened its jaws and yowled. The Medjidie priest.

Talon fingers of the man's other hand clutched Peter Scarlet's arm.

It was touch and go for Scarlet right then. He could scarcely see in the dark and splash, but he saw well enough to know this shrieking priest would drown everybody if those fingers weren't out of his beard. The little curio hunter had not been a sailor for nothing. Bringing up a fist like a bludgeon, he cracked the old Moslem's jaws shut and the creature folded up in the water. As if three broken ribs and a five mile swim weren't enough, he had a Moslem holy man in tow.

Peter Scarlet got a fist in the old man's hair, and swam. Ten strokes farther he knew he was finished for good. Every pounding wave almost broke his back, and he sank twice with the priest dragging like an anchor on his arm. Blowing water, he gained the surface and paddled in a dark like the Last Day.

Wind screamed at his doused head, his towing arm was unjointing at the shoulder-socket. His chest seemed to burn inside him. He could feel the eyes jutting from his face. He knew he had swum a thousand miles and he knew he hadn't floundered thirty feet. He was glad of one thing, though, he whispered up to his fainting brain. His final act he was delighted with. He had dropped a bullet square to the middle of that Russian skipper's head.

FOAM BATTERED at his face, and his mouth was under. But something round and white whirled up from the spume and batted Peter Scarlet in the nose. Dragging his free arm from the flood he got an elbow into the floating object. Then he freed his mouth of water, and he laughed. When he did that a few stars twinkled out in the sky and a faint light lit up the sea. Peter Scarlet got his arms through the round white object, and yanked the old priest's head clear of the water. Then he laughed again and struck out.

When that ship's rail had crashed it had taken a life preserver overside with it. The little curio hunter's arms were through that hoop of white cork now. He could see the name stamped on the canvas binding, read the letters by the star-shine. *The Little Flower of Mercy.*

But even with that cork supporting his armpits it was no bathing-party swim to they Turkoman coast. Peter Scarlet had to keep kicking and he had to keep his hands on that Medjidie holy man. Tons of water caught him, flung him high, plunged him into roaring black valleys. The valleys avalanched and flung him starward; spindrift knifed at his face. His hands went dead with fatigue. His back was twisted like a bedspring. The chill got into his veins and plugged his eardrums, and his chin kept clacking on the life buoy. The clock was slow on the Caspian Sea; he seemed to have floated for years.

But the tide was with him that night, if the time wasn't. The little curio hunter and the Medjidie priest were rushed along in a sweeping current; a following sea that hurled them down the hills of water and slid them over the crests. It was five miles further and five hours later and shortly after midnight when the little American curio hunter and the mummy with the Order of the Medjidie turned turtle in a combing breaker, rolled through a swirl of liquid and sand, and went acrobating with a cork hoop up a beach.

A slim sickle of butter-yellow moon had just knifed clear in the indigo sky. The wan rays slanted down a humpy ledge of cliff behind the beach and washed with pale violet the forehead of a mammoth limestone rock that bulged like an enormous blister out of the sand. Lucky for Peter Scarlet and the Moslem that the wave had not hopped them into that curve of stone. But they missed it with room to slip a piece of paper in between, and bounced down on a fan of sand where the driftwood lay like mounds of old dead bones.

PETER SCARLET spat a dank matting of weeds from his beard, and unbent his back with a groan. On the sand beside him the Medjidie priest began to writhe. The little curio hunter wriggled out of the life preserver, pushed up on wobbly knees, leaned over the holy man and pumped on the creature's ribs.

A mechanical wheeze blew from the mummy's sucked-in parchment cheeks. He groaned. The green eyes opened. He sat up. Those eyes flickered green flame at Peter Scarlet. Moaning gently, the old holy man fumbled his dripping chin. His face was violet in the moonlight, and sitting there among those bony sticks he looked like a Djinn from Gehenna conjured from shadows by an Asian charm.

"You," he whispered suddenly at the little curio hunter, "you once more saved my life." And then he whispered something that made the little curio hunter sit back on the sand with a bump, mouth open, eyes wide. "And for that you shall be rewarded, *hazoor*. For that you shall be well repaid. I saw you listening on the boat, *hazoor*. Listening while I beguiled my foolish sons with the story of Jenghiz Khan's ghost. I was watching your face, little friend, and I saw perhaps you had believed. Do not tell me I read your thoughts wrongly, *hazoor*, when I guessed you would give your soul to see the ghost of the long-dead Khan, to see the crown of emeralds...."

To see the crown of emeralds! A heat rushed through Scarlet's brain. The ancient priest's voice rose needle-sharp in the moonlight. "And because you have saved my life, *hazoor*, I will reward you with a sight that few men in Allah's world have ever seen. I will show you the ghost Khan, *hazoor*, I will show you the emerald crown of Jenghiz Khan."

Peter Scarlet opened his mouth, but no word could come out of his lips. This old Medjidie priest was promising to show him the crown of Jenghiz Khan, to prove the reality of Asia's most famous legend, give him a look at a treasure that thousands had hunted in vain, that seven tough adventurer's had cruised into oblivion to find. The holy man had guessed it. He *would* have sold his soul to see those gems.

"Listen!" panted the priest. And Scarlet listened. Wind sang around the limestone rock and sent spirals of dust down the shore. Tumbling water played an undertone, and the old priest's voice came chanting down the moonbeams to clutch the night in its spell. The green eyes glimmered and the thin hands waved; and Peter Scarlet sat in the driftwood like a thing of stone. That old priest was telling again the story of the mighty Jenghiz, and telling it in a way to make the minnesingers and troubadors of old Europe look tongue-tied with nothing to say. Now his voice was an organ playing storm, now a crying soprano violin. His waving hands reached into the past for pictures and his voice filled the beach with color and fire and noise.

Scarlet saw the conquest of Asia take place on that lost, lonely beach. He saw the terrible Jenghiz with his Golden Horde gallop roughshod down Asia's plains. He saw the flash of scimitars, the scatter of warm blood; heard the screams of defeat and the triumphal cries of the conquerors. From China to the Caspian Sea the great Khan swept all before him, and there on his head where all might see to know, mighty Jenghiz wore the crown of emeralds that flashed like the stars of Allah's sky.

THAT OLD priest was a master storyteller, and he brought the sweat rolling down Peter Scarlet's cheeks. When he told how mighty Jenghiz came one night to that Turkoman valley he had Peter Scarlet crouching like an electric spring.

"And mighty Jenghiz, walking alone, came to a lake where the waters boiled forever and the waves were of steam and a miracle of fire in water could be seen. The Khan was frightened for the first time since his birth, for surely here was an omen. But Allah spoke and the Khan dropped dead and his ghost walked from him into the scalding lake and wearing the emerald crown. But when the voice of Allah halted, mighty Jenghiz rose again, and fled. But there stayed the ghost with the crown, and there lives the ghost to this day. And when the moon of Allah comes and Allah speaks, the ghost of Jenghiz rises from the boiling flood, the emeralds in his crown, and laughs to tell Allah of the glory that shall come once again. I have heard the laugh. The emeralds, thanks to Allah, I have seen."

It was quiet on that little neck of beach when the Medjidie's voice stopped then. Too quiet. Peter Scarlet's words came out of his beard like pieces of heated metal. "You say the place is near this coast?" he panted. "And you will show me the ghost—the emeralds? Where?" he panted. "Where…."

"Not far," the old priest whispered, his green eyes shifting up the cliff behind the shore. "I have been on this very spot before. I recall this cliff, that sandstone rock. The lake of fire is not distant to the south. You shall see the ghost and the emerald crown; thus shall I reward you for my life. But no Unbeliever can stay to hear the laugh, for that Unbeliever should die."

"I want to see the emeralds," Scarlet cried. "Those gems that are brighter than stars, brighter than sun on the sea. Just give me a look at that emerald crown, that's all—" By heaven if there really *was* anything behind this old codger's yarn—"You give me a glimpse of those stones, old boy, and I'll let this ghost take care of itself. You *saw* the crown?"

"I saw, *hazoor*." The mummy creaked up to its feet. "And you shall see, too, by my faith. We can start now, *hazoor*, and, by Allah, I will show you the way." He pointed at a crooked path belting its way up the cliff. "We follow the trail from there, my friend. It is not very far."

The Medjidie took a step toward the trail up the cliff-wall, and then stopped short in his tracks. A burst of red fire lanced from the rim of the big limestone rock. A roar tore echoing and booming up the coast. A bullet sped through the startled moonbeams and clipped a thread from Peter Scarlet's elbow.

CHAPTER III

GET THE YANKEE

MOVING LIKE A released spring, Scarlet snapped the Luger from his hip and fired. The night shook with the thunder. Splinters of lime flew from the rim of the big rock. The ricochetting bullet took a shadowy head square between the eyes and caromed into the brain. The head squawked, spattered and vanished. But spurts of red fire leapt all along the rim of the rock. The night crashed and slammed as a spate of hot bullets screamed criss-cross over the curio hunter's head. Bounding like an antelope, Scarlet dashed for the shadow of the cliff where the screeching Medjidie waited.

A chorus of savage howls went up from the fortified enemy. A whirl of lead chased Scarlet as he ran. Bullets bit into the cliff and brought down showers of gravel. Scarlet flattened himself against the dark stone. Ahead of him, on the sheltered trail, he could see the old holy man dancing. The limestone rock on the headland had started to blaze like a corn-popper, and a fusillade ripped across the beach, seeking the curio hunter.

"Down!" Scarlet yelled at the Moslem priest. "Keep down, old one. Who are these fiends who try to ambush us?"

"No brothers of mine," the old man chittered above the gun-roar. "By Allah! no son of Islam dares live on this haunted coast. They are spirits, *hazoor*. Devils come from hell. Ghosts of your own *feringi*...."

Crouching, Peter Scarlet emptied the Luger at the limestone rock—four shots rewarded by four screams. With flying fingers, he jammed another cartridge clip into the smoking chamber. Bullets whined over his head with a chilling *roooom* and dug into the cliff. Ghosts never fired pistol bullets like that. Devils from hell, all right. And the little curio hunter recognized human howls in a dozen tongues.

He crouched on the trail at the cliff-base, trained the Luger on his knee, and gunned a salvo down the rim of the rock across the beach. Answering gunfire chipped pebbles over his head. A crisscross of flames zaffed over the rock's broad rim. The roar of gunnery echoed away and away down the ragged shore. Tinted gun-smoke billowed across the little beach and bulged up at the moon. And the wind whisked them away.

Those men weren't Moslems, at that. The old Medjidie priest was right. *Feringi.* White men. The little curio hunter could hear them shrieking oaths above the blatter of their guns. German, French, Polish, Greek profanity. At least a dozen of them behind that boulder. "Get him," a French voice screamed in Russian. "After him, you dogs. Get that Yankee jackal. He's up there on that cliff. Charge."

"They're coming," the priest wailed in Scarlet's ear. "See...."

"Run," the curio hunter shouted. "I'll cover you. Get me out of here." It was no place to linger with that limestone rock spouting men like a hive spouts hornets. Shadows were slithering over the rim, screaming, dropping to the sand below. Gray heads came flickering through the smoke. Fire lightninged through the uncertain haze. Body doubled in shadow, Peter Scarlet swept the beach with a scalding fire.

Shadows shrieked, spun, dropped, but others came on, pumping long rifles and waving long knives. Moonlight caught the shine of twisty, wet faces, the glint of cruel blades, the gleam of gun-barrels. On they came through the fogging powder-smoke—twenty of them, straight for the spot where Scarlet waited. A bullet scissored through the curio hunter's beard, and another ripped a scorched rag off his sleeve. Peter Scarlet didn't wait any longer. Cold sweat beaded out on his forehead, and, doubling low to the ground, he galloped up the trail after the priest.

Those men were advancing like wolves. The trail zigzagged

up the precipitous rock-shelf. The curio hunter and the old Turkoman holy man bounced over rocks, dashed up a path of sharp stones, cut through masses of bramble and thorn. Scarlet would stop, crouch, and fire downhill; and the priest would blunder and skip ahead. "This way." No time to load a cartridge clip, and Scarlet had to save his fire. The wolves in pursuit were shooting all over the cliff-face, but it only needed one lead slug to stop a man.

JUMPING, DODGING, waltzing through briar and brush, Scarlet followed his ancient leader up an escarpment that didn't want to be climbed. It was no trail to run with bare feet and three cracked ribs. No trail to be raced by a half-drowned mummy and a little curio hunter melting to pieces with fatigue. Only the superb marksmanship of the Luger was saving the day just then. Those tigers in the rear were learning respect for that sharp-shooting pistol; didn't want to close in too soon.

Knocking sweat from his eyes, Scarlet could see the ghostly figures below, a gorilla band darting in and out of smoke and gloom, piercing the sky with frenzied yells. *"La Bas.* There he goes— That Yankee. Get him— Shoot, fools. That bush up there— Don't hit the priest. Get the American— *Herr Gott,* is one man stopping us all?—Quick. After him. Catch him—" Gunfire and screams and the sound of trampling boots, and mad bodies charging through brush.

"This way," the Medjidie shrieked; and Peter Scarlet raced between two blue boulders at cliff-crest. The priest threw a shaking hand at a narrow defile knifing its way inland into darkness, fled up the cleft.

Cursing, Scarlet dropped to his knees for another shot. The Luger spat fire and down the hill a shadow went bouncing. It leapt to the beach below, rolled on the wood-scattered sand. Down there the beach was tiny, and from cliff-top Scarlet could see beyond the giant limestone rock. He could see the coast curving northward, a dim horseshoe, and the sea beyond was an ocean of creaming ink. The headland shut off a further view, but Scarlet had glimpsed enough. There on the other side of the big limestone rock, a white bumboat lay empty in the thin lace of surf. These wolves had sneaked up in a small boat.

White flame blazed up from below. A boulder behind Scarlet's elbow went to pieces with a smash. Scarlet's Luger gave a futile click. No time to load just then. The Medjidie was vanishing up the dark defile, screeching at the curio hunter to hurry. Cursing, Scarlet spun on heel and ran. But he had just had time to glimpse a face come plunging out of shadow down the cliff path. The face had wild eyes and an evil, red welt across the mouth. The face of the sailor Rachmaninoff had chased across the deck of *The Little Flower of Mercy*.

RIGHT THEN, Peter Scarlet, the little American curio hunter, knew he was in for plenty. The crew of *The Little Flower of Mercy* had jumped the ship and rowed ashore.

They'd been behind that giant rock when Scarlet and the Moslem holy man had tumbled up on the beach on the other side. They'd heard the old Medjidie telling his story. That riffraff scum of sea garbage had heard the story of the emeralds that were bigger than stars; had heard the Medjidie chant that he knew where those emeralds were. It needed no master mind to imagine how that pirate crew would want to see those jewels for themselves. And they wouldn't want a little American curio hunter in the way.

"Hurry," the old priest shrilled. "Follow me." It was no easy place to follow anybody. Dead rock reared in fantastic shapes on either side of the defile. Cones of pale moonlight slanted down the rock, shed a confusion of purple shadows and wrought an eerie pattern on the uncertain path. Wind from the sea caught funnels of dust and sent them dervishing at the indigo sky. But where the moonbeams and shadows failed, the landscape was gray, unreal, dim as a faded photograph. The Persian mountains to southward made a caravan of stone elephants against the horizon. Here the world ended, and here it had begun.

It seemed to the running curio hunter that no man had

hustled up this scene since Allah first tossed it there in anger and called it Turkestan. The cries of the ancient priest were the first ones to echo up those crags. The smash of the Luger pistol shattered a silence that had lain unbroken since Time began.

A maroon boulder heaved up in the shadowy path. Peter Scarlet dived around its crest and fired at shadows crowding up the trail. The answering gunnery rattled the sky. Lead whistled like a river flooding up the defile. The shadows scattered and howled as Scarlet raked the path with a fast salvo. "Stopped 'em that time," he yelled at his companion. "Come on, you curs," he screamed at the pursuit. "Come on, an' die."

They bunched together and came, drilling the night with bullets and screams. The shells flew from Scarlet's Luger like popping corn. Ramming in a fresh clip, he dodged low and sped after the fleeing holy man. Another hundred feet up the narrow cleft and they were skipping through a litter of massive, round stones, granite white, cobalt blue, limestone, sand red. Some giant had been playing marbles with boulders and strewn a handful in that arroyo. The priest and the little curio hunter scrambled among the rocks, heard bullets smashing stone chips behind them.

"AFTER ME," the priest yowled; and they turned up a corridor that led into a cul-de-sac of crags, clefts and rock crannies that would have baffled a jackal. Leaping along like a dried monkey, the old Moslem darted under a ledge and tagged back into the defile again. They could hear the sailors baying along behind, hard on their heels.

Side by side, Scarlet and the priest skirted another clutter of colored boulders and raced across a sandy bowl under shadow of a steep ridge. The priest was beginning to pant like a leaky engine. Peter Scarlet ached in every muscle. There were red smears where his bare heels left tracks in the sand. Hanging against a smooth ball of stone, he groaned for breath. The priest had halted, bent low to study the dark path. The pursuing sailors were spilling out of the rocky corridor, filling the dark with savage yells.

Suddenly the old Medjidie jumped at Scarlet. He dropped tight fingers on the curio hunter's arm. "We are not far," he squeaked. His green eyes were brilliant in his knotted face. "The lake of fire is near. But there will be no place for concealment." A sharp explosion on the ledge overhanging above them cut off the priest's gaspy words. A gargled cry burst from the ancient's mouth. A colored bubble shimmered on his writhing lips. Crimson enamel welled out of his ear and washed down his corded neck. His fingers clawed. His knees buckled. His green eyes sparkled, and he collapsed with a thud to the sand.

A mad oath blew from Scarlet's teeth. Pressed against the rock, he swung the Luger and sent a scythe of steel at the ledge above. A little bouquet of white smoke tarried there; but the old priest's killer had gone. And the wolf-gang of sailors from *The Little Flower of Mercy* were charging among the boulders like a raving surf.

Bullets trilled over the curio hunter's shoulders as he stooped and dragged the dying Medjidie into deeper shadow. The priest's face was twisted to parchment now, great sweat beads watering his withered forehead. His breath was coming like steam as Peter Scarlet fought to stem the flow from his drilled neck-nape. The pale green eyes were bright on Scarlet's face.

"I'll get him," the curio hunter sobbed with fury, bending over the dying Medjidie. "I'll get that devil who killed you, old man. I'm going after him—"

The bubbling lips murmured. Peter Scarlet stooped low to catch the words. "My friend—you see emerald crown—go tonight while moon of—Allah shines for you. See." The green eyes glimmered. The wet mouth smiled. "Take every red stone—to the right—and—you come to—fiery lake. See mighty Jenghiz—ghost. But do not stay. If ghost laughs you—would die."

The green eyes flamed and went out. The mummy lay still.

SCARLET SPRANG to his feet. Every red stone to the right and he would reach the legendary lake. But he'd get the hound up on that ridge, first. Dropping two fast shots to hold back the gang on the rim of the sandy bowl, Scarlet flung himself into the shadow under the ledge, raced among the boulders, climbed a crag of stone and, belly to rock, crawled up to the shelf whence the murderous shot had come. But the murderer had fled.

Now the sandy bowl below was rioting with the sailor mob. A fence of spectral figures, they charged across the bowl, sweeping the scattered rocks with a scalding rifle fire. A false move in this situation and Scarlet knew he was done. Where had the gunman on the ledge gone? Back of the shelf the cliff shot up like flat board to the ridge. The killer must have slithered off the other edge of the shelf and rejoined the mob below while Scarlet was listening to the old priest.

A fox with its back to a wall had better chance than the curio hunter, then. No way off that shelf and those pirates howling across the sand beneath.

"Steady!" Scarlet snarled at himself. Taut as steel wire, he crouched there on the ledge, gun a-swing in a wet fist. Directly below the ledge a Negro danced, shotgun in one hand, crooked dagger in the other. Scarlet could see the face that glistened like a chunk of coal, the bulgy goo-goo eyes. The bulbous eyes rolled up at the ledge, and the black pirate caught the glint of the Luger. His mouth opened like a pink cave and his yell brought the gang of tigers on the run.

The gun in the black's fist jumped to an ebony shoulder. But that gun never went off. *Wham! Slam!* Scarlet's automatic belched twin flames. The bulbous eyes disappeared in the coal-chunk face. Scarlet threw himself flat and rolled aside, just in time to escape a savage fusillade from the rest of the crew.

He sniped another face from the swirl below. Then the Luger clacked empty, and Scarlet shot a hand to his bullet-belt. And a cold sweat spread down his face. Only one clip of shells left. Six shots. And more than a dozen of those panthers charging the ledge where he lay.

Wild figures swarmed up the little crag. A deafening fire broke from the guns of the assaulting gang. Moonbeams flashed on jagged knives. Teeth glistened pearly in ugly masks. On either side of the shelf those sailors from *The Little Flower of Mercy* attacked.

A half-naked figure with the face of a gorgon swung off the crag and flung himself at Peter Scarlet. The curio hunter fired into that gorgon face. The gorgon flopped, rolled from the ledge, dropped ten feet to the sand. A hurled knife crooned under Scarlet's chin. Hot lead screamed past his face. He fired to catch the next man climbing at him.

Then the iron handle of a stiletto, thrown at rocket speed, slammed into Scarlet's temple. The wicked blow flung him back on his heels. Losing balance, the little American curio hunter reeled off the ledge and dropped into the hands of three screaming sailors who had waited on the sand.

CHAPTER IV

STRANGE RESCUE

BITING, CLAWING, STABBING sharp blades, the three pounced on the curio hunter like maddened animals. But Peter Scarlet was a little mad himself. His gun blazed. The remainder of the crew, leaping down from the ledge, struck into a one-man tornado. Fists going like wheels, gun roaring, the little American curio hunter was the vortex of a cyclone that whirled across the sandy bowl. Four shots, and he made three of them good.

A knife gashed his chin. Fingers fastened in his left arm. He struck out with the gun-butt and smote the sailor with the bruised mouth between the eyes. A muscled sea dog with the face of a Malay got an arm-lock clamped on Scarlet from behind. Scarlet's feet shot up in the air, came down on a crumpled body; twisted under him. The Malay got teeth into Scarlet's right shoulder, and the pack fell atop him with a victorious howl.

"Don't kill him," a harsh voice screamed. "Save his throat for later. The priest is dead. We must make the Yankee show us the way to the treasure."

"Slay him," a Frenchman yelled. "Let me get my knife at him. We can find the emeralds for ourselves."

A squall of approval went up from the pack. Thick hands trapped Peter Scarlet's throat. Boots stamped on his ankles. He saw a ragged Spanish dagger come sneaking through a tangle of arms, horrent heads and kicking legs. Wet bodies drove his back into the sand. The breath had gone from his lungs.

The knife made a cut at his exposed jaw. But that knife never got home. Suddenly the pack chorused a terrified squall, flew apart like leaves in wind. Those sailors sprang off Scarlet's prostrate figure, screaming. Down the wind came a weird, fearful battle-cry: *"Allaah! Akh-baar...."*

Those sailor ruffians from the fo'c'sle of *The Little Flower of Mercy* went bounding among the boulders when they heard that yell. As if some monstrous genii had told them to scram, and they were scramming for all they were worth. For one second Scarlet lay panting, groaning, astonished, that wild call of Islam ringing through his stunned head. That call had come from the corridor in the ridge. Next minute its source appeared. A white cloud swept into the sandy bowl. A white cloud of robes that bannered in the dust, bobbing hooded heads, flying sheets. Scarlet glimpsed brown, yelling masks, dark eyes fierce with hate, dark-skinned hands that flashed evil blades moon-shaped and thin little Arab daggers. *"Allahu Akhbar!"*

"The pilgrims," Peter Scarlet grunted. "The pilgrims from the boat."

Yes, the pilgrims. That mob of Turkoman devotees swept over Scarlet like a raving *jehad,* but they didn't touch the curio hunter. A joyful yell blew out of Scarlet's beard. Those Moslems were going after the sailor crew. They were demons of Mohammed's vengeance, white lions in a fog of dust.

Peter Scarlet guessed what had happened. Those pilgrims had seen Rachmaninoff, the Russian, knock their Medjidie leader overside. They had seen the little white American go to their holy man's aid, and shoot the Russian in the head. Then those pilgrims had decided to go after the Russian's wild crew. But the crew had jumped the ship. And the furious pilgrims had manned boats on their own hook and followed the crew to the shore. Peter Scarlet was mighty thankful, right then, that he had wanted to help that wretched old Medjidie. The pilgrims had found the dead body of their holy man, and their yowl of rage soared up to the sickle moon.

One of the Moslems leapt at Scarlet, knife upraised. Then he stooped and hauled the curio hunter to his feet.

"It is the good *Roumi*. Our friend of the Faithful. By Allah, let no man among us touch a hair of this man's beard."

THE FOLLOWERS of the Prophet gave a barbaric cheer and left Peter Scarlet standing in a swirl of hot dust. The hurricane of blowing robes, shot through with the lightning of sharp knives, went shrieking into the boulders where the sailor gang had fled. There sounded a frenzied crackle of gunnery; but those fo'c'sle dogs couldn't stop that pilgrim mob. The night was alive with the screech of wild conflict.

Mouth agape, half stunned, Scarlet watched the sailors who had tried to murder him go racing—a jackal band—around the rim of the sandy bowl. The pilgrims of Allah were the tigers now. Hoods and white robes streaming, they chased the jackal crew across the sand, routed them back down the narrow canyon and into the cleft in the ridge. The sailors shrieked in fear.

The corridor echoed with a din that clamored fainter and fainter and ever more faint among the dim escarpments and crags. Sailors and pilgrims had vanished out of sight. Once more the landscape was a fading photograph, unreal, a confection of shadows and moonbeams, quiet as the dead among its colored boulders save for the few, thin shot-echoes that came dimly from far away.

It had happened too suddenly for the little American curio hunter to believe. But there he stood alone, panting, rubbing an aching hip, a cold Luger automatic in his sweating hand. The same crescent moon was still cruising the sky, and his shirt still dripped water from the Caspian Sea.

Peter Scarlet touched his face to see if it was there, shook a numbed head to clear a swimming brain. Suddenly his eye fell on the body of the old Medjidie holy man, spraddled, silent, beside a rock. Wizard words whispered again through Scarlet's mind: "It is not far. Take every red stone to the right and you come to the fiery lake. Go tonight—while the moon of Allah shines."

Tonight… Not far… Every red stone to the right. An oath speared from Peter Scarlet's teeth, and he began to run. At the eastern rim of the sandy bowl a flat, red rock jutted from violet glooms. Beyond the rock a gaunt gully bent its way into darkness under the ridge. The little American curio hunter skirted the rock and turned to the right.

With caution, yet swiftly, he made his way through the dark.

QUEER, THAT feeling that he was being followed. He had found seven of the red boulders lying within a hundred rods of each right turn, marking a trail through canyon and dry watercourse. And at the seventh he had stopped, ducked into shadow, certain that something was sleuthing his trail. Nerved like a drawn wire, Peter Scarlet clutched the Luger, pierced the landscape, sharp-eyed. No living thing could he see.

"Nerves," he growled to himself. "I'm strained to nothing. If I don't find that lake pretty soon I'll be jittering like a kid in the dark.…"

Listening, he could hear no sound. The Turkoman pilgrims must have chased those wolves from *The Little Flower of Mercy* into infinity. This Turkestan coast was pretty close to world's end as it was. A good place to tweak the nerves of an image.

Stone crags lifted fantastic outlines against the stars. The moon was a thin silver blade on the edge of a green-hued cloud nest. Silence rained from the sky and poured up out of the rocks and breathed with a soundless wind that crept around stone corners to finger Scarlet's face. His bruised foot moved a pebble, and it rolled with a loud noise.

"If this keeps up," the curio hunter jibed at himself, "I'll be believing every word of that old mummy's yarn. Good place for ghosts to kill men by laughing. But that emerald crown may be around, at that. That superstitious old priest said he saw the gems. By heaven, that *is* something moving back there."

But he saw it was only a shadow growing longer as the moon retired behind the clouds. Dodging around the rock, he jogged up the dim trail, urging his feet along by means of mental visions of emeralds the size of stars. Moslem legendry always involved a lot of ghostly yarn that was nonsense, but emeralds were emeralds. Jenghiz Khan had dropped that crown of his somewhere, and that old Medjidie priest had seen it. He wouldn't have told a pure lie to a man who'd just saved his life.

"Emeralds," Scarlet panted. "The yarn dripped truth."

He plunged down a dark ravine, measured the turn on another of those preposterous sandstone boulders, stumbled up a narrow chasm flanked by high escarpments. Filtering through cloud, the moonlight was a weak and phantom illumination. The trail was faint. The cliffs on either side were spectral, and the climbing path made a ghostly stairway toward the stars.

THE LITTLE curio hunter picked his way up the twisty canyon, stopping twice among pooling shadows to look back nervously, certain he had heard movement other than his own. No sound, then, save his own steamy breathing, the creak of his battered bones. Quiet? The North Polar wastes were roaring Times Square compared to that patch of Turkestan. Then his taut eardrums did catch a sound. An odd, indefinable echo that seemed to drift from beyond the crest of the rise he was climbing.

Peter Scarlet hung on his toes, listening. The devil, what was that sound? His own escaping breath? Or the hiss of leaking steam? That was what it was. The bubbly sound of hot steam, the churn and fizzle of boiling water. White with astonishment, the little American curio hunter sent a needle-eyed glare up the mounting path, and thought he saw beyond its rise a faint and wavering mist.

A gasp burst from his stiffening beard. "The lake. The fiery lake."

Getting his legs to pump under him, he sprinted up the path, topped the rise. At every step the bubbly, steaming noise gained volume in his pounding ears, and when Peter Scarlet gained the crest of the canyon trail and saw what lay beyond, his jaw flew open with astonishment, the eyes bulged in his head, his feet stood rooted to earth, and he forgot the sensation he had suffered—the feeling that someone was haunting his rock-marked trail.

CHAPTER V

THE FIERY LAKE

BOILING LAKES WERE phenomena not new to Peter Scarlet, the little American curio hunter. He had seen them before in the western United States, in South America, New Zealand and the Hebrides. But never before had he seen one the size and fury of this witch's cauldron that bubbled and simmered and fumed, a scalding pool, locked among those lost Turkestan crags.

Perhaps a quarter mile in width, the lake lay above sea level, heaving against its rocky shore. Hot waves dashed against the crags and exploded in bursts of steam. Steam blew from the combers, hissed from every drop of the tortured, bubbling surface that would never be still. White steam rolled in writhing clouds along the wind, whistled from every crevice and cranny in the jagged rocks of the shore. The noise of the cauldron beat from rock to rock. Water smashed, jolted, spouted and squirmed, in an endless and futile fight to escape a subterranean heat mysteriously generated beneath the lake bottom.

In that God-forgotten landscape of rock and shadow, faint-lit by a wan Asian moon, that scalding, agonized water pan, sulphurous and founting, was the very doorway to Hades. Blistered waves and scorched stone. The very ledge on which Peter Scarlet stood awestruck spat rags of steam from a thousand cracks. A wet heat blew in his face and a hot fog wrapped damp coils about his head. That witch's cauldron was Paradise Lost. That shouting, boiling lake was a brew of liquid souls condemned for hell.

But what planted the little American curio hunter with the cold sweat creeping from every pore was the strange raft that lay stranded on the rocks where he stood. There it was. A raft.

A bit of human handiwork tossed there to make him wish he were not alone. Five logs of olive wood bound together with thick hempen strands.

That raft sprawled on the edge of the steaming beach with hot water lapping at the hewn log ends. Peter Scarlet stared with steam-bleared eyes. The hawser strands binding those logs were almost new. And that round, white object lying solitary on the raft's rough surface....

An exclamation of wonder whispered from Peter Scarlet's stifled tongue. "A sun helmet."

It was but three steps to that abandoned raft. The rock was hot underfoot. It took Peter Scarlet a long time to get there and the soles of his feet were chill on the steaming stone. He didn't feel better with that sun helmet trembling in his hands. The band of the helmet fell to pieces at his touch, and its crown was sopping and rotten. But he felt as if he'd picked up a skull. The cloth shell was worse than a skull. That sun helmet stood for a white man, and where had that white man gone?

PETER SCARLET swept the lake with an unhappy eye, stared at the frantic sweep of water. The helmet in his fingers made a punky taste well in his mouth. The steam was like sulphur in his nostrils. Some white man had built a raft to shove out on that boiling flood.... The raft and his helmet had returned.

The crags along the cauldron shore seemed to groan. The steam cried out as it soared up through the shadows of night; hung in cotton-thick, swirly banks to hide the center of the lake. The little American curio hunter stared at the whirling steam cloud and a burst of spray flew up suddenly to take him in the face. That water was hot enough to cook an egg.

He wiped his eyes with a quivering fist, stared again through the steam, and *saw*. Then Peter Scarlet yelled. The relict sun helmet fell from his hand. An icicle slid down his spine. Sweating like a bridegroom he stood, unable to stir. But how he yelled.

For the moon had escaped the cloud bank and a shaft of amber moonbeans dropped out of the sky to fall like a stage-spot on that wild lake caught in the crags. At the same time a wind blew out of the canyon behind Scarlet and cleared the cauldron of steam with a flying gust.

The steam clouds blew to silvery rags. The lake surface leapt into view.

And there in the middle of the scalding flood stood a mammoth, phantom figure with arms outspread and a face that was a gray blob and a body that melted into the heaving water like a skirt of milk. Water glimmered and poured from the ill-formed shoulders. Steam wreathed the figure with a ghostly mist, bulged like smoke from a crack across the formless face. A steaming, granite statue. That was the thing Peter Scarlet saw in the middle of that storming water.

But that was not all. That preposterous, faceless head was a steaming, steaming blob, but the crown atop that head was no blob. From where he stood, paralyzed, Peter Scarlet could see those emeralds set in that hoop of gold. A crown on the head of a specter. A crown of emeralds the size of bird's eggs. Emeralds that caught at moonbeams and fired darts of green light at the sky. Emeralds that winkered and blinkered and blazed livid green, and shed weird rainbows through hot steam. Emeralds that rivaled the glory of Allah's stars.

The lake snorted hot steam and the wind puffed it away and the awful thing across the boiling water never stirred and Peter Scarlet stood on a beach of hot rock and yelled at an emerald crown. Something had to happen right then. And something did.

Iron arms shot out from behind and snapped on Scarlet's wrists. A bulk of damp flesh crashed against the curio hunter's spine and flung him face down on the rock. A voice like a saw on teak-wood grated above the hiss of steam. "I've got you now, you murderous little slob." An oath. "You and your treasure, besides—"

Steel hands cranked Scarlet's head on his neck, twisted him until his shoulder blades rammed against the rock. A face looked into Peter Scarlet's and voiced a guffaw. A face too small for the size of the body, with eyes like rancid dots to port and starboard of a jutting nose, and a bushy black beard on the jaw. On the nose was perched a dainty pince-nez with a gold chain anchored to one ear. And the head was bald with a pinkish scar across the scalp and an ugly red gash in the middle of the skull. The Russian skipper of *The Little Flower of Mercy*… Rachmaninoff.

CHAPTER VI

DEATH'S LAUGHTER

RACHMANINOFF SNARLED AS he drove his knees into Peter Scarlet's chest. "I've got you. Where I want you. Bones of a Cossack, yes. You are surprised, my little cockroach? You thought you had killed Rachmaninoff? You never thought a cold plunge would revive me, eh? You didn't think I would climb back aboard my ship and get my sailors and row after you. Ho, ho!"

Blindly the little curio hunter struggled, but he couldn't move that iron-muscled hulk. "Ho, ho!" Rachmininoff was bellowing. "And we found you there on the coast, my dogs and I. And did I hear that old flea-bitten holy man tell his story? I did. And I ordered my little devils to capture you both, which they did not. Lucky for me I went up on that rock ledge to try at sharpshooting. I made a mistake when I killed the priest, but fortune was with me. Had I not climbed among those crags as you came up to find me the Moslem curs would have found me as they found my crew. Then I should never have been able to trail you to this place where the stone image stands in the lake. And what fine emeralds they are, eh? Fine emeralds."

A mad light blazed from the eyes behind the delicate glasses. "What gems they are, my friend. Ransom of forty kings. And all for me. All for Rachmaninoff. Do not try to struggle, little one. Cry out as you please. Your Moslem friends are far, far away. And I see you have here a little raft to ferry me out to that stone idol so that I may take the gems. Splendid." Rachmaninoff's hairy fists tugged at his belt, yanked loose the leather strap.

The little American curio hunter choked. What was the fiend going to do with him? Working fast, the Russian lashed Scarlet's arms behind his back. A knife glittered in Rachmaninoff's fist. Ripping a strip of cloth from Scarlet's shirt, he laced together the curio hunter's ankles. Then he towered above him, grinned down in Peter Scarlet's face.

"See now, my friend?" He drove a foot into Scarlet's hip. "See what happens to those who try to play with Rachmaninoff. I should love, my little sparrow, to heave you into this scalding pool, here. You would cook, eh? Yes. And I would enjoy the sight. But I must row out to those emeralds, you understand. And with the treasure in my pocket, then I will let you lead me back to the coast. Unhappily I do not know the secret of this trail which the old Medjidie whispered to you. You will take me back to the coast, eh? And then I will have time enough to think about disposing of you. Ho, ho. The rich Rachmaninoff will take his time, so."

Dealing another kick at the prostrate curio hunter, the big Russian made a leap for the raft of logs.

SWEAT RAINED down Peter Scarlet's cheeks, and he cursed himself for not heeding his instincts when he thought somebody had followed him up the trail. He sweat a little more when he remembered the bullet he had fired at this Russian skipper's skull. "I'm mad," Peter Scarlet whispered to himself. "Mad."

And that was a madman's picture—that boiling crag-locked lake, that impossible stone image in the lake's foaming center, that fabulous emerald crown perched rakishly on the ghastly, steaming stone head. Bound and squirming on the rock-ledge shore, Peter Scarlet was a madman. He could feel the heat of boiling water in his face, could hear the roar of the cauldron. And the incredible Russian skipper was a madman, lunging to heave the raft of olivewood logs into the steaming flood.

"Go," Rachmaninoff screeched, and the raft lit into the water with a splash. A sheet of steaming liquid fell on Scarlet's cheek and he yelled at the burn. Rachmaninoff screamed a laugh as the raft floated clear in the foaming lake. He spat a curse of triumph at the curio hunter on the shore, and his face was knotted with lust as he pointed a finger at the image across the foam. "See. Those emeralds. All mine, you little cur. All mine." His voice roared loud above the hiss of the boiling waves.

The moonbeams danced on his pince-nez glasses and made them glisten like tiny satellites. His bald head shone like a knob of polished brass. The pink scar was livid on that burnished skull, and the raw, fresh wound in its middle glowed like a tiny flame.

"I will be back soon and a *bon voyage*," he bawled at his captive. "I will come back rich, little Yankee. Ho, ho, I see you looking at your pistol."

Darting across the rock, the Russian kicked the pistol a savage boot. The Luger went slithering. It lodged among sharp rocks at the rim of the ledge. "I shall watch you as I sail, my friend. Make one move toward that gun out there and I shoot your shoulder off from where I cruise. I will give you back your gun after you return me with my emeralds to the coast. Perhaps I will give you the bullets in it, too. After you've guided me back to the coast, of course. I will leave you the bullets to pry out of your leg." Rachmaninoff saluted and bowed. "And now—" he grinned—"to pluck the gems—"

Snatching up the battered sun helmet that Scarlet had found on the raft, the Russian sprang for the boat of logs. Strange sights Peter Scarlet had seen in his day, but never one as strange, as mad, as nightmare-wild as the sight of that giant Russian kneeling precariously on that raft, shoving off from that steaming ledge of rock that made a beach, and paddling into the lake by means of that awful sun helmet.

He roared with laughter as he paddled, and the raft blundered slowly across the bubbling water. Scooping at the hot waves with the sun helmet, Rachmaninoff ferried the raft across the steaming foam. The little curio hunter could see the bald skull glistening through the steam. He could see the glint of the pistols jammed in the Russian's waist; could see the evil glitter of the pince-nez glasses on that Blackbeard face.

Chill sweat rippled down the curio hunter's cheeks. He could not strain at his bonds. He could not cry out. He could only balance on an elbow and watch the raft crawl out across the cauldron. The moonbeams shed a witch-light down the crags and tinted the steam. They made to shine the shapeless image in the center of the lake; made to shimmer that emerald crown. And there was that raft propelled by the muscle of mighty arms and the scoop of a vanished man's sun helmet, slowly, ponderously, cruising the devil's own pond. Hot water fumed and splashed around the raft. Once raft and Russian vanished in a cloud of steam. Then wind whipped the steam sky high, and Scarlet saw the nightmare ferry and its demon passenger had nearly reached the goal.

RACHMANINOFF LET out a yell when the raft's bow touched the image of stone and steam; and the little American curio hunter yelled, too. Peter Scarlet yelled again as he saw the big Russian slice a strip from his pant-leg, fashion a strand of rope, knot it through one of the hawsers binding the logs, and tie the raft against a knob in the stone monster's misty base.

Wide-eyed and gibbering in his beard, Peter Scarlet watched Rachmaninoff balance at the raft's edge, grab a handhold on the image, and swing up on the stone. The Russian was small on that monstrous thing, and he looked no bigger than a chimpanzee as he started to clamber its bulk. Water burst and exploded and steamed beneath his heels. Steam wreathed his striving body. Pop-eyed, Scarlet watched from the beach where he lay marooned, and the hammer of blood in his brain almost drowned the squall of the lake.

And it seemed to Scarlet that the lake was squalling a louder pitch at every moment. Rachmaninoff's figure inched up that preposterous statue out there and the water roared louder and louder. Even the rock under Scarlet's body seemed to tremble with the noise, and a few stones came gamboling down the crag where his gun was lodged. Waves burst against the beach and showered Scarlet with stinging spume. The lake surface rolled and the raft tied against the distant image tossed high in the steam.

The little American curio hunter's tongue dried out in his mouth. A shout blew up from his lungs. Rachmaninoff had an elbow crooked over the image's outstretched arm. He reached a paw at the emerald crown flashing above.

But something was happening. The lake was booming and a waterspout went twirling along its crest. Through the mist of founting foam and steam, Scarlet saw that the ghost of stone was not as tall as it had been. The base had *gone*. A tremor shook the rock under him and the lake tilted with a wild tide. Waves lashed the beach and a strange, fantasmal thunder crackled among the crags. And then Peter Scarlet froze to a block of ice.

For a terrible, disembodied sound chattered out of the crack in the stone idol's face. A plume of steam rushed from that crack and that spine-freezing sound rushed out with it. A laugh if Peter Scarlet had ever heard one. A crackling, snappering, steaming halloo that yah-yahed up at the sky and boomed off into the night. A hurricane swept the lake clean of mist. The surface bucked twice, flinging scalding froth high in the air.

The curio hunter heard a Russian shriek go wailing away and away on the wind. He saw the ghostly stone image go down like a plummeting star. A geyser of boiling water towered, founting, where the image had been. For one awful split-second a tiny figure hung kicking on the tip of the fountain. Then the fountain fell down and the figure fell with it. And the scalding waves closed over with a furnace roar.

The image with its emerald crown was gone. Rachmaninoff with his pince-nez glasses was gone. Only two things lingered, out there on the tossing spune. A foundering wooden raft. And the echo of a terrifying guffaw.

CHAPTER VII

THE RUSSIAN'S SKULL

PETER SCARLET, THE little American curio hunter, got back to the Turkestan coast. He had managed to work his hands loose from the leather belt that bound them. Then he took every red stone to the left, and he reached the coast of Turkestan just as the sun was charioting its crimson path up out of Asia's east.

He found a mob of Turkoman pilgrims holding prayer meeting there in the dawn, and they seemed more worried at the sight of him than at the crowd of dead sailors stacked up like cordwood on the sand beside them. The little American curio hunter didn't care about those things. He wanted to get to Abassabad, and the pilgrims took him there. He never could remember the journey. Far as he knew he slept most of the way and a couple of the Sons of Allah carried his slumberous body.

He found the British consul in Abassabad and he told the

British consul most of the story. The British consul said "Jolly good" and "capital" and rubbed manicured hands together and poured Peter Scarlet a "dashed strong noggin of Holland's." He was a good fellow, the British consul. He'd been in the East long enough to know two and two didn't quite make four, and he told Peter Scarlet he believed the story. He poured another long one for the little American curio hunter, and took him into the consular library.

"Don't tell the yarn in America," he cautioned, kindly. "They won't believe you. They never saw Turkestan. They never saw a monk with green eyes. The only old emeralds they've ever seen were in Tiffany's window. And they don't know how the moonlight out here can make a ghost of gatepost. You have to see one of those boiling-water lakes to believe in it. I know.

"Sometime in the long ago an ancient barbarian found that lake and got the brainy idea of building an idol to his god. Perhaps there was an island in the middle of the lake and he set the stone idol up there. That Turkestan country has a bloody queer way of jolting and shoving around, too. Seismic disturbances. Little earthquakes, see? Probably that island with its stone image has been jolting up and down out of that lake like an elevator for the past thousand years.

"Few hundred years ago Jenghiz Khan walked up to that lake, spied the image and thought he was seeing his immortal soul rising from the steam. Knocked together a raft and poled out to crown his spirit with his emerald headpiece. When he got back to the shore the ghost had sunk. There you have it. A few Moslems have spied the thing and cooked up a jolly lively legend. As for the laugh you heard, it was nothing but steam roaring up through that stone god's cracked insides. I suppose the moon hits a certain phase and the thing heaves up top for a spell, then sinks again. Just happened to get your Russian daredevil at the right moment, same as it got those others who tried to snatch the gems.

"Don't tell your yarn to the folks at home," the friendly consul cautioned again, "or they'll think you've had one too many."

"Thanks." Peter Scarlet smiled. "You've helped me keep clear of the asylum. I thought I had both feet in the violent ward."

BUT THE little American curio hunter never told the British consul at Abassabad the entire story. He didn't want to strain the fine threads of credulity too much, and he didn't tell about the shot he took at Rachmaninoff's bald, scarred head. For many days afterward he would draw the Luger from his belt and stare dully at the blue steel automatic. That Luger of Peter Scarlet's had never missed a mark, and therein lay a fly in the ointment.

The little American curio hunter took to dropping in on local bars and rendezvous and sitting with the gun on his knee and drinking a little too much. Always he would toss his last one with a shake of his trim white beard. "By heaven, I *did* see the wound in that infernal bald head. Even if the bullet hit a glancing blow it would have split open his brain."

"What the devil," asked a companion one afternoon when they were sitting in a veranda café at Tiflis, "what the devil are you muttering about? Posing that pistol on your knee and mumbling to yourself?"

"I'm thinking," Scarlet confessed, "about a demon named Rachmaninoff—"

"Rachmaninoff?" the other barked. "You don't mean that big Russian skipper that disappeared somewhere in Turkestan? He's been wanted by the police around here for months. They've got his mug plastered up around everywhere. Look. There's the notice on that wall."

Scarlet followed with his eyes the pointed finger and saw an old poster going dim against cobwebby boards. The photograph was fading, a face with whiskers on the jaw, hairless pow, and pince-nez balanced on nose. But the fading words beneath slapped Peter Scarlet's eyes:

"Wanted for Murder. Feodor Rachmaninoff. Distinguished features: black beard when last seen, pince-nez spectacles, bold, unusual scar on skull from operation, as large portion of skull-bone was shot away during World War naval engagement, and heavy silver plate inserted beneath....

Peter Scarlet slapped his Luger pistol, and clapped it on his hip to stay.

TOWER OF DEATH

Once Peter Scarlet's vigil slackened—and the Turkoman struck. For it was written that the little American should find what he sought in the Tower of Silence—where only the dead may enter.

"MURDER," SIGHED MAQBOUL el Mussulmanni, sadly petting his crimson beard, "grows more difficult every day. In the old days it was merely a matter of bullet or blade. Or if one were more subtle, a drop in a cup. But now—"With mournful eye the Turkoman watched green lights shimmer in the emerald on his thumb, and one judged from his tone that a depression had hit the Persian border.

"No longer can honest Moslem chiefs dispose of foes and breathe a prayer to Allah and forget it. But the white men come to harry, pry and accuse; and to remove a man in secret one must hide well the deed. The major problem in murder nowadays is not how to kill your man, my son, but how to hide the body. You understand, my son? How to hide the body."

Not legally recorded as anybody's son, Hamid the Humpback poured hookah-smoke from his Persian beak and nodded. "The police have been troubling you again, *hazoor?* They still seek that Englishman we disposed of but four moons ago?"

The Turkoman nodded with a sneer. "They seek him still. Four moons ago they came sniffing, found nothing, and went away. They discovered no body; therefore they discovered no evidence. But they still hunt the body. They know the Englishman, Smith, never got out of this town and they believe I had something to do with it. Now there is one among them who guesses too much, by Allah!" Maqboul el Mussulmanni stroked his beard. "That one must also die."

Hamid's deformed shoulder shrugged gently, and he reached for the jar of cloves. "That Englishman with the pane of glass to his eye was an easy fool to kill," he chewed. "And we shall kill another white man?"

"With pleasure. But this one is not of the British police, just a busybody who sticks his snout in business not his own. A white fool from America, my son. A sly little merchant with a beard and pale eyes who calls himself nothing but a curio-hunter—"

"*Rahmet Allah!*" The hunchback glared nervously around the smoky, rug-hung room. "You mean the little Yankee who will call here this very evening about a matter of buying some pearls—"

"Do you think he comes about pearls?" the Turkoman snarled. "Did he blind you, too, with such a tale? No. He comes not to buy, but to spy, I tell you. A friend of the British police he is, and also a friend of that Smith whose skull we crushed and whose body we hid so beautifully. Listen. He comes to find that body. By the back teeth of Allah, his wish shall be fulfilled."

Smoke eddied from the hunchback's mouth. "We murder him—"

"As easily as we did that other; and foil the police once again. Could they convict me before? No. Because they could not find the Briton's corpse. Nor shall they find the body of this Yankee."

The Turkoman made a glide across the floor and his lieutenant in crime-mixing felt a shiver go up his zigzag spine.

Maqboul el Mussulmanni hauled aside the curtains of a window. Outside the sun was westering in a sky of rose. Dusk like blue liquor lay soft on the flat roofs of the town in the valley, and the hill beyond was a naked, five-mile sweep of sand, empty and barren. Not quite empty, though. Distant on the horizon stood a lonely, white, round tower of faceless masonry. A flat-roofed cylinder of stone without visible doors or windows or purpose, squatting dim in the dusk. But three black specks drifted high above against the sunset.... Buzzards. The tower had a purpose for those buzzards. And a purpose for Maqboul the Turkoman.

"The Parsee cemetery, little cockroach. The burial tower of death. And tonight there is to be another Parsee funeral. Does my plan become clear?"

"Clearer than a sorcerer's crystal," smiled the hunchback. "Then we do the same with this Yankee as we did with the silly English fool."

Maqboul's red beard sighed softly. The gem-garnished thumb touched a thin, green grin. "Not exactly the same. The English fool went there dead with his head broken in. The Yankee shall go there alive. He shall go as his friend went—with honors— but he wishes to see that friend's body, and he shall. We shall use drugs. And before this curio-hunter goes to burial I shall tell him how and why he dies and make him sorry he came to spy on Maqboul el Mussulmanni, most powerful of Turkoman chiefs. You recall how we handled the Briton? The Yankee must be downed the same way, only do not slay him with the first blow, my brother, do not slay with the very first blow. Let him die of remorse and the buzzards and thirst. By the sunshine and hunger, my brother."

Hamid the Hunchback, who was nobody's brother, grinned.

"He comes within the hour," Maqboul purred on. "So go behind the curtain and wait the signal as before. A light blow on the head, then leave the rest to me. I want to tell him what is going to happen to him, old cockroach, make him suffer the more. You recall the proverb? 'He who knows he is about to die, dies twice.'" Maqboul el Mussulmanni belched a chuckle, reached for the gilded zither at his elbow, eased back in the cushions and thumbed a twanging chord from the strings. "The Yankee shall die those two times—"

TWILIGHT WAS oppressive. It seemed to the man riding the roan pony up the trail that dusk had done little to ease the heat which had burned down the valley all day. A relief to get through the scribble-scrabble welter of the border town, but the slope was lonely in a silence that had pooled there since Jenghiz Khan's Golden Horde had gone away.

The little American curio-hunter mopped sweat from his leather forehead; glared about him. That little white tower across the valley gave him the creeps. A Parsee cemetery. "Towers of Silence" they called them. The Parsees wrapped their dead in white linen and laid them out in those towers for the birds to eat. Novel, but a trifle gruesome. Gossip had it that only certain Parsee priests knew how to get in and out of some of those towers. They never seemed to have doors.

Peter Scarlet shrugged and spat. Who'd want to go near such a thing anyway. He'd always steered clear of them, and he'd better keep his mind on the business at hand. Uneasy, he dropped a hand to the Luger on his belt. You never could tell what crazy Moslem might be hiding behind a rock with a rifle that ached to go off. Bad country, this. And the Turkoman chief knew he was coming, too. You never could tell—

"Rottenest skunk in the Orient." That was the way Major John Burnt of the provincial police had described Maqboul the Turkoman. "Treacherous as a cobra. He has a gang of cut-throats ready to stab for him all the time. Don't take your eye off that snake for a second. I'm bloody positive he had something to do with Smith's vanishing up there in that town. He'd been robbing from a British expedition, and we sent Smith up there to get a bead on him, and I know confounded well he found Smith out and did him in somehow."

"Grant Smith was one of the best friends I ever had," Scarlet said, thin-lipped. "I'm going up the border and find out what became of him. I'll get the hound who murdered him if it's the last thing I do. I've heard of this Maqboul. Sells pearls and whatnot. Opium runner and all the rest of it. And if he killed Smith—"

"My last shilling on it he did. My men found proof that Smith went up to the Turkoman's place. Wasn't seen again. But the blighter says Smith never was even there. And we haven't a shred of proof. There isn't a trace of poor Smith in all of Persia. Poor devil. Can't even locate that fool monocle he always wore. By heaven, I'm certain this Maqboul had something to do with it."

Peter Scarlet turned his pony up a path leading to the house of Maqboul the Turkoman.

FLAT WHITE walls blank as the face of a liar loomed behind a garden of rhododendrons. Blue shadows lay in wells under a peepul tree and streaked with darkness an arched doorway done in amber tiles. The little American curio-hunter fingers on the handle of his guns. He dismounted and strolled to the door.

For some reason the sweat began to coast down Peter Scarlet's cheeks. He saw a curtained window and knew unseen eyes were peeping through folds of dark cloth, watching his movements. With an effort he dropped his fingers from his gun-butt; lounged to the shadowy doorway.

Somewhere inside the house a zither was being strummed, and the nervous notes trailed through arched halls in tooth-chilling discord. Scarlet shoved the sun helmet to the back of his head, spat through his snowy beard, and slammed a fist on the doorsill. You had to bluff these Moslem curs.

Shadows moved at the end of a corridor as a curtain silently parted. The curio-hunter caught the picture of a squat Moslem with a bulbous green turban and a crimson beard sitting cross-legged among a lot of blue cushions like some manner of poisonous vegetable sprouted among fat leaves. A zither strummed in his lap. A pious smile appeared in the red whiskers.

"Aye? It is the American come to call about a matter of pearls? Enter, *hazoor*. My poor house, everything belonging to Maqboul el Mussulmanni is yours. *Salaam, sahib*. Yours has been a happy journey today?"

"A long ride," Scarlet said grimly, crossing the threshold to enter the rug-hung room. "But I'm sure it'll bring me success. As I let you know, I'm here to make a bid for those famous Kurdistan pearls you advertised in the Alahabad bazaar."

The Turkoman bobbed his turban and a gentle note twinged from the zither's strings. The gentle note ended in a blinding crash. Wind whizzed behind Scarlet's back. There was a half-second's smell of cloves. The little American curio-hunter spun on heel with a shout, yanking his gun; but the lead club struck him squarely on the temple and he whirled in a tangle of curtains, robes, crooked arms, snappering teeth. For a moment he was on his knees.

A hunchbacked gnome came out of a red swirl, lashing down again with the bludgeon. The club smashed Scarlet's fingers and his gun went flying. Howling an oath, the curio-hunter struck back, fists going like wheels. The room spun and the hunchback shrieked. Quick as had come the unexpected assault, Scarlet had had time to duck the fatal blow. But the club had stunned him, and blood poured into his eye. Locking an arm around the crippled Moslem's throat, he flung him across the room.

Hamid the Hunchback hit a wall with a smash. Wood splintered. Plaster fell in a dusty shower. Whipping blood from his face, Scarlet dodged the flung leaden club; rushed. A zither struck his jaw with a wild *thrumm*. Maqboul the Turkoman sprang from the cushions with a yell. Flinging an iron fist, Scarlet took the Turkoman hard in the mouth. Maqboul el Mussulmanni somersaulted over backwards, spitting teeth and screaming to Allah.

Scarlet's feet tripped in a tangled Bokhara rung. His boots

shot out from under him. And Hamid the Hunchback, leaping like a panther, snatched the club and brought it down on Scarlet's neck-nape.

"**KILL HIM!**" Hamid the Hunchback waved twisty hands, and streaked the gloom with crackling Persian oaths. "Kill the dog, now. Let me slay him at once, *hazoor*. The man is like a tiger. If he gets loose—"

"He cannot get loose, fool!" Maqboul the Turkoman was surveying the knots lashing together the little American curio-hunter's ankles and wrists. A moan escaped Scarlet's lips, and he writhed, spraddled on the floor, striving to blink red mists from his eyes and move his hands. Maqboul el Mussulmanni drove a kick at the curio-hunter's hip. "He can never get loose. An elephant could not break those lashings. They will be there when the Yankee is nothing but white bones—"

"Would he were white bones already," the contorted Persian cawed, fingering his swollen nose. "By the beard of the Prophet, I do not like this, *hazoor*. You mean to send him to the Tower of Death not dead, but drugged in sleep. Suppose he works his hands free. Suppose—" the thought brought sweat sprouting on Hamid's inhuman brow—"suppose he gets out of that tower, *hazoor*."

His mind clearing from the fogs of blinding pain, Peter Scarlet dimly heard the words of his captors. They had tied him down. The tower. They were sending him, drugged, into that Parsee burial tower. The words bit into his spinning mind, cleared his head, and sent cold ice through his veins. The Turkoman's voice came louder and louder.

"You speak like a vendor of parrots, old one. Like a Hindu without courage to eat meat. He cannot untie his hands; those thongs are like steel. If he did get free of the tower what could he do to me? My men would slay him on sight. But he cannot get out of the tower, old roach—"

"I'll get out." Heaving his shoulders, Scarlet rolled his frame across the floor, opened his eyes and stabbed his captors with a savage glare. "I'll get you for this, Maqboul. The police will swing you for this if I don't kill you first. Send me to that tower, if you wish. But I'll live to kill you if it's the last thing I do." His eyes met Maqboul's, coldly defiant.

Maqboul el Mussulmanni's laugh was like the rattle of pebbles in a brass can. His eyes twinkled an evil glow to match the wink of the gem on his thumb-ring. He spat through his crimson whiskers and grinned at the little American curio-hunter trussed on the floor. Even the humpbacked Persian's criminal spine could shiver at the Turkoman's voice. "Your talk is big, you white pariah and eater of scum. It is like the talk of that Englishman who came here to spy on me, before. That white *feringi* named Smith, with the pale face and the circle of glass to his eye. Ahee. Perhaps you knew of him?"

The room was a smoky red cave striped with grotesque shadows. The men standing over Peter Scarlet seemed to be gnomes. A patch of dying twilight fell on the curio-hunter's face; found it twisted and wet. His voice was hoarse in his snowy beard. "Maqboul, you jackal! What did you do to Smith, you—"

"Hamid hid behind the curtain from, which he struck you down tonight," Maqboul purred gently. "He also struck down your friend Smith. The blow crashed the Englishman's skull as it would have crushed a pecan. A neat blow. The white fool fell without even breaking the glass in his eye; without knowing what hit him. He was dead. With kindness in our hearts we buried him." The Turkoman smiled venom. "You shall find his body, *sahib*. You wished to see it. Maqboul will show it to you."

Scarlet's voice came brittle through clenched teeth. "You'll die for this, Maqboul. You murdering rat, it'll take the police about five seconds to pump you full of lead. They know where I am—"

"THEY KNEW where the Englishman was, too," the Turkoman advised sweetly, patting his beard. "But he vanished, you see. You, also, shall vanish as did the other one. They shall never find your body, *sahib*. Only the Parsees may enter the Tower of Death which stands on yonder slope. Listen, little one. Tonight the Parsees have a funeral for one of their sect. Today an old cameleer of the Parsee faith was bitten to death in the *serai*. At this moment he lies wrapped in white linen in his house, waiting the march to the hill. There shall be a disturbance near that house, my friend. A fight in an alley. Merely a drunken tribesman dealing blows to a Parsee mourner, perhaps. But the Parsees shall leave the corpse a moment, and your own linen-wrapped body shall be substituted.

"I tell you this, my friend, because you shall lie sleeping in drugs at the time; and I wish you to know what will occur. We leave one eye free of the shroud so you may see when you wake, however. And when you open your eyes you will find yourself alone in the tower of the dead. Alone and tied in knotted bonds and wrapped in spotless linen. Look around you, my curio-hunter. See the bones nearby. The sun will be hot in the sky. Dust you will see, but no water. Meat, but none for food. Vulchers will float overhead, waiting, waiting. Finally they will attack. Then remember how you came to spy on Maqboul. Ahee. And before you die look carefully around. You will find, then, the friend whom you sought. You will find him in the Tower of Death."

Desperately, Peter Scarlet sought the littered floor for sign of his gun. It had gone. Hamid the Humpback had drawn from his robe a bolt of white cloth, and something shiny appeared in the hand of the Turkoman. An open window behind showed a patch of star-scattered sky and a slim, yellow slice of a moon, sailing in hot silence.

"You dogs!" Scarlet choked out. "I'll get the two of you—"

"Kill him, *hazoor*." The curio-hunter's steel eyes made the humpbacked Persian's face go pale. He turned on his master with a whine. "He will become conscious in the morning after the dope has lost effect. What if he gets free of the tower—"

Maqboul el Mussulmanni shook his red beard; smiled at the green fire on his thumb. "Nobody gets free of that tower, my friends. Only the Parsee priests know the secret of how to enter and leave. I with all my Moslem spies have never found the doorway. The mourners carry the corpse to a tunnel and leave it there. The priests spirit it away. The tunnel ends before a monster rock, ten feet thick and one hundred feet high. How do they pass the body through that barrier? None but the Parsee priest who watches the tower can know. Once gone beyond that rock under the tower no body has ever returned. And by tomorrow night this American will have died of heat and thirst; the vulchers will have dined well on his—"

With a furious yell, Scarlet hurled himself doubled across the tiles. But Hamid the Hunchback was on him at a bound, smothering him in white cloth. Bent fingers stuffed a rag through the curio-hunter's teeth to stifle his voice. Iron hands pinned down his shoulders. Blind, ice-hearted, fighting, the little American curio-hunter strove to throw off his assailants, but he could move neither hand nor foot, and a white linen strip was slowly winding about his kicking legs.

Maqboul el Mussulmanni held high a small metal object. He knelt beside the curio-hunter with an oath.

"A Parsee burial," he cackled. "Ahee. The police will never find you, little Yankee. If they find a dead Parsee in the river it is nothing to them. They seek you with your pig's blue eyes and white beard. But you will be in the Tower of Death, with one eye looking for your friend. The drug in this needle will keep that exposed eye shut with sleep until dawn, and then it will awaken. And you will find yourself buried with your friend, little skunk, and you will die soon after. What a jest!" The Turkoman's eyes shimmered green, and his parroty laugh chittered through the gloom. "You are buried first, and die second."

Peter Scarlet, the little American curio-hunter, groaned. Hamid the Hunchback snickered. Maqboul el Mussulmanni laughed, stooped low, and jabbed the shiny needle into his victim's arm.

SOMETHING WAS doing in the Lane Of The Cameleers. Shadows plunging from wattle doorways; swirling together in dark corners. Hoarse shouts. Muffled blows. Clang of knife on knife. Feet pounding through darkness. Black dust. A whirling stew of bumping bodies, tossing Moslem turbans, dodging Parsee caps. "In the name of Zoroaster! That faithless Moslem struck a Parsee priest! Down with the Mohammedans!"— "Drunk he was. Hit our priest in the doorway of a house of mourning. Thrash the scoundrel."

Raging Parsees poured from the doorway of that "house of mourning." Slim Persians in white caps and fluttering gowns, bent on punishing the offending Moslem. The offending Moslem shrieked for help, and his friends came running from every quarter. In half a second the lane was broiling with the fighting mob. Parsee mourners charged, to do battle.

And in that house the linen-wrapped body of the dead Parsee cameleer lay alone on its mat.

A candle shimmered faintly at the foot of the silent white figure. Friends and relatives of that still white figure were battling like fury, now, some distance from the house. The dead waited alone.

Suddenly it was not alone. Soundless shadows slipped into the dim-lit room. The faint candle-beams caught in outline a fat, green-eyed face with a bushy red beard; a squat, humpy body with the back of a zebu and the countenance of a fox. A linen-wrapped body was slung like a meal-sack between this uninviting pair. The red beard whispered, steaming.

"Fast, Hamid, before the fools return. Lay him on the mat. So. Hurry. Give me the feet of the corpse. Now then—"

"Master, it is perfect. They will never suspect robbery—"

"You are a fool. A fair exchange is no robbery."

A fair exchange. The shadows slithered from the room. Black shadows slid back into place. The candle flickered on, undisturbed. On the mat lay a still, white figure, wrapped from foot to head in spotless linen. If the windings of the shroul were not bound as tightly about the head as they might have been, allowing one closed eye to peep through when it should waken, there was nobody to suspect or notice. If the figure on the mat was breathing, it breathed too faintly for suspicion.

Certainly the returning Parsee mourners never suspected. Returning to their funeral, flushed with the triumph of having routed a Moslem gang of hoodlums, they sat around that still white figure and calmly resumed their masks of woe. At length the priests were back to preside.

The still white figure was lifted from the mat with reverent hands. Slowly the Parsees filed from the little house. Slowly the procession moved up the night-hung valley toward the silent burial tower. Only the two priests carrying the body knew the secret of entering or leaving that age-old Parsee cemetery. But no man in that funeral march ever guessed that the figure they carried so sadly across the sand was not a brother of the faith died of camel-bite, but a little American curio-hunter tied hand and foot and sleeping in his shroud.

THIRST. THAT was the first sensation telegraphed to Peter Scarlet's stunned brain. Thirst in his rag-stuffed mouth.

The next thing he realized was that he was being carried. He couldn't move. The dope was still logy in his veins. He could not open his eyes. But he could feel the hands on his shoulders and feet; feel himself swinging in air. Horror clutched his heart with iced fingers. This was the funeral. They were carrying him to the Tower of Death.

Far-away voices whispered like echoes from a vanished yesterday. A dank wind seemed to penetrate the cloth windings that masked his face. A faint smell of sweat and smoke.

With a desperate effort of will, the little American curio-hunter opened an eye. Cold darkness swirled about him. But somewhere far ahead a torch blinkered in a smoky murk. He knew he was being carried through an underground tunnel. If only he could move his head, move a foot, get a yell through that gag in his teeth. But his muscles were lead and his head was a chunk of cold stone.

The drug surged through him again, and he felt himself

creeping into a well of chill unconsciousness; a drowning sea of night. With fighting fury he strove to drive the drowsiness from his mind. But he was in a dream, a nightmare.

A long time they must have carried him. There were two of them, by the sound. The one at his feet carried the torch. Two Parsee priests. And they were toting him through a tunnel.

Peter Scarlet dreamed. When he managed to open his eye he was floating through Stygian dark. Twice they dropped him to the ground, and stood gasping. One of them growled in Persian: "Who would have thought the old scoundrel was so heavy?" How the little curio-hunter fought to make a noise, battled to move. The effort weakened him to sleep again. Once more hands were lugging him through the dream, and finally there was a curious episode of nightmare.

It seemed as if the priests had come to a halt. "Here is the rock," one of them whispered from far away. His companion was grunting strangely.

Next minute the darkness was full of a weird hissing, swishing sound. Chill breezes smote viciously through the shroud wrapping his body. A cyclone had come into that subterranean night. And, bound as he was with ropes, linen and drugs, Peter Scarlet suffered the terrifying impression that an enormous object was streaking with great speed past his face; some huge, unseen obstacle going by in the dark like a loosened hurricane.

It was part of the nightmare, yet it was real, for one of the priests panted: "Watch out, my brother."

"The number is thirteen," came the strange reply.

"*Thirteen!*" the first voice screamed. Hands snatched at Scarlet's numbed shoulders. Jerked off the ground, he felt his paralyzed body flung soaring through the air. One terrifying split-second he felt something shoot past him like a planet shrieking through space. Then hands caught him and dragged him head-down and bumping up a flight of what seemed to be steps. The sound of wild wind died away.

A hot, stale atmosphere stifled Peter Scarlet's breath in his fainting lungs. The hands loosed him with a bitter Persian oath; dropped him on warm stone. Footsteps trailed away and were gone.

The little American curio-hunter was alone. Dope reeled through his brain and stunned him like a heavy blow....

A savage ray of sunlight burning through the cloth on his face awoke him. With a start of white terror he remembered, and opened his eyes. One eye was unmasked, enabling him to see. Peter Scarlet opened that eye, and found himself staring at a human skull.

ONE THING Peter Scarlet knew. He must keep his wits about him; save his mind from flying to pieces; fend off the icy terror that threatened to freeze the springs in his brain and snap him stark crazy. From Azerbaijan to Keijo, from the Caspian to the Sea of Japan the little American curio-hunter had cut his sign. No clement meadows in between. Paths across the Orient chopped out of wildest adventure. But never in his life had Scarlet dangled by so thin and fiendish a thread as now.

Tied helpless by merciless thongs, wrapped in a shroud, gagged, laid out on a shelf in a Parsee burial tower with old bones for company. A dawn sunshine like a furnace blast baked the eyes in his head. At noon that sun would be like livid fire. And the vulchers....

Already the black specks were floating high in the metal sky above. Fury shook Scarlet's trussed frame. That Turkoman who could conjure such villainy had murdered Smith. The curio-hunter had a vision of the tall quiet Englishman, forceful and ironic, with a monocle to his blue eye. More than once Smith had shot gun to gun with Scarlet in those little scraps men run into east of the Suez Canal. But the honest English policeman had been no match for the Turkoman and his deformed geni.

"I'll kill them!" Scarlet moaned to himself. "I'll get out of this. And I'll get my hands on that Maqboul's throat—"

But rage was useless. It tired him out. Groaning, he reopened his eye, heaved his head up off the stone. Beads of sweat poured out on his bandaged face. He was lying on a stone shelf. A plaster wall sheared up at his right; straight up one hundred feet skyward like the wall of a prison. At his left the shelf fell away in a series of ledges, like seats around an amphitheater, or a football stadium.

Merciless sunshine flooded the tiers of shelves. And every shelf was crowded with mounds of white bones. Human skeletons laid out in serried ranks…. Hundreds of them, side by side, row on row in neat alignment on the ledges.

Gagged and bound in that cocoon of linen, Peter Scarlet was lying on the top ledge, marooned in that cemetery in a corner of Persia which had been forgotten for five thousand years. Silence and bones and heat.

A black shadow swept suddenly across the wall and a vulture came coasting by for a look, talons hooked. Peter Scarlet's one exposed eye glared his terror, and the vulture drifted away. The sun was like a knife in his eye. He moved his head, trying to relax, fighting for calm. In a heat that would bite through a pith helmet, he had little chance with his head protected by only thin linen wrappings. With a burst of fury he strove to move his arms and legs, but they were pinned tight in the cloth, like dead weights. By heaven, was he going to die on that shelf in that ghastly repository of bones? Maqboul had done him in with Satan's genius. But he wasn't dead yet—

Peter Scarlet shrieked and could make no sound. He squirmed and writhed and the silence burned hot around him like a pall. Even if he did work loose he could never scale that wall. He remembered the Turkoman's smooth reassurance. No man save the Parsee priests knew the secret of that tower's door.

The sun…. How long could he fight that sun?

A whirr of wings reached his ears, and a black monster fluttered over his face. He could see the vulture's eager talons, the bead-quick red eyes. Scarlet lifted his head an inch, and the bird flapped away in surprise. A moment later it was back with a companion. They hovered like two demon clouds; then swooped.

Claws, yellow and sharp, tore at the cloth on Peter Scarlet's chest. He lunged a shoulder. The birds shot away and a little swirl of feather's settled on Scarlet's stomach.

A WAVE of terror and rage such as he had never known boiled through Peter Scarlet's helpless body. He struggled, straining every muscle; bit at the rags in his teeth; flung his head on his neck in a wild effort to shake the blindfold free of his left eye. The cloth and the cords were tight.

Whirrr! This time there were more wings than before. Scarlet heard them coming, and waited with his stomach knotting under his belt. In a squeaking, reasty rush the birds plummeted down, charging to the feast. Scarlet's shrouded body was enveloped under a tumult of fighting claws, tearing beaks, beating wings. Biting, tearing in a cloud of dank feathers, their crimson turkey-necks and dark wings in a heinous tangle, the vultures settled on Scarlet's frame. And Peter Scarlet battled with every ounce of power left in his stifled soul.

Only one move could he make; and he threw himself into it like a madman in a strait jacket. Heart pounding fire, brains frozen in his scorched head, Scarlet rolled. Smothered in that awful storm of claws and lusting beaks and whirling feathers, the linen-wrapped body of the curio-hunter turned over on the shelf. He heaved his shoulders; twisted; fought. The bird-mob shrieked on top of him as he lunged. But he rolled down the shelf, and bumped over the edge. He landed with a back-breaking slam in the heap of bones on the shelf below.

It had only been a drop of three feet. Then the birds were on him again. Under pounding wings, he heaved himself over among the dry bones, and rolled for another edge. Like a mummy going down a flight of steps he bumped to the third ledge, praying only for a long drop that might kill him. But the cloth that wound him helpless served to save the smashing of his skull.

The vultures followed his ghastly flight.

Bruised, beaten, smothered, Peter Scarlet rolled on down

the tier of stone shelves, with the birds screaming over him, white bones scattering under him, the mind going to pieces in his head. And finally he came to a ledge where the drop was five feet to the shelf below. The birds were at him like animals, and the little American curio-hunter did not hesitate. With a groan he heaved himself over the edge; went smashing to the stone shelf beneath. Body doubled, he struck the ledge. Gray dust spouted up around him. Those bones down there had been pulverized with age and he had landed in a three-foot thick blanket. Somehow he pulled and tugged himself out of the dusty mound, across the shelf where the bones were newer, to the last ledge of them all.

The crash of his fall had sent the birds off in terror. He could make the last ledge. With a heart-breaking heave, he flung himself at the rim, twisted his head and glared down. It was a long straight drop to the stone floor at tower bottom. Thirty feet. That would be all right. Slowly he swung his legs around to get them over. He was not afraid. With what mind he had left he told himself that he had played the game and deserved this chance to die by his own doing. Peter Scarlet humped his shoulders, trying to make them turn. In the effort he swung his head; and a sheen of steely light caught him like a needle in the eye.

Lying on the rim of that last fatal drop, Scarlet caught his muscles taut with a jerk, and, cheek against stone, stared.

A blazing, fiery eye stared back into his swollen one. A disc of glass, ironic in the face of a yellow skull. *A monocle!* The roof of the skull was broken in, and the demon sunshine, slanting through that hole in the bony shell, came streaming out through the glass set into the eye like a ray from a white-hot torch.

That clear shaft of heat seemed to wash like daylight into the little American curio-hunter's mind.

"Saved! Poor old Smith! But I'm saved."

HE ONLY waited to chafe his wrists, and stoop down to say good-bye. It had been an easy matter to burn through his bonds in that point of sun heat. Later they could come back for Smith.

"And, anyway, he died in the house of the Turkoman," Scarlet whispered to himself. "And I'll get him for you, old man," he promised out loud. "I'll get him. You gave me the chance, and nothing on God's earth can stop me now."

Kicking the charred cloth from his boots, the little American curio-hunter began to run. Burns on his ankles couldn't slow him. Nothing would stop him now. He pounded up the ledge, a solitary figure in that resting-place of bones. Running was not easy; his legs were like rubber at the knees and he wanted to sit down and sob. But the dynamite in his heart served to move his numbed feet. A tiger's laugh blew from his beard when he saw the arched corridor leading under the wall below the ledge.

Scarlet shouted as he ran. "They must have carried me in here. There were steps. A tunnel. Something that flew like a gale in the dark—"

The little American curio-hunter yelled when he found the steps under the wall. He laughed when he found the mouth of the dark tunnel winding down into the ground. Fists knotted, beard streaming oats, he pounded down a subterranean passage, and the dark was cool on his face.

Suddenly his run was stopped. An enormous shaft of stone, gray in a light that drifted from a distant overhead cranny, barred his path like a wall.

Not one man nor a thousand men could have lifted that giant sledge of stone. Peter Scarlet stopped short in his tracks with a cry. Dim words scattered through his head. The strange nightmare he had dreamed in his drugged sleep. The impression of a hurricane in the night, a huge object speeding past his face. One of the Parsee priests screaming out: "Thirteen."

Thirteen…. With a cry, Scarlet flung himself at the stone barrier. The great face of granite seemed to move. He heaved with all his might. The giant block whispered in the gloom and trembled on its base. Straining every nerve 'til the sweat bubbled down his cheeks like hot drops of wax, Scarlet pushed against the massive rock. And it slithered like a sliding door into the

*Scarlet's brain reeled as one of the loathsome
creatures settled on his chest*

dark wall. He glimpsed a sliver of black tunnel beyond; then the rock shot back across his path at express train speed. But the little American curio-hunter had the secret.

"Balancing rock."

A balancing rock set into a crevice cut across the middle of that tunnel was the secret those Parsees had known. Scarlet threw himself against the slab, and the huge granite mass slipped over in its socket; shot back in a rush of dark air. One, two, three. The massive rocking-stone rolled over and whizzed back.

A baby could have tilted that stone had he known himself able to move it. But it would take more than a baby to leap past the whizzing rock at that second when it lay over on its side and the way through the tunnel was cleared. That stone swung into the cleft in the wall and came back flying; lightning tons of granite that shot back into place with a grinding smash.

Scarlet threw aside the stone and it hurled itself past him like a triphammer. The curio-hunter heard himself counting above the roar of the wind. Four, five, six. At thirteen would the stone swing in its longest arc and give him the longest chance of jumping through? He would take the chance, anyway.

"Thirteen!" he shrieked, heaving at the swinging slab. The slab whistled over on its base, and Peter Scarlet sprang.

THE TURKOMAN with his green turban and crimson beard sat cross-legged among the cushions of his rug-hung room. This was the hour he enjoyed. After dinner, with the scent of his flower garden perfuming the warm twilight. And tonight the great Maqboul was more than content. His men were in the valley waiting a rich prize.

"My men?" he wheezed in his buttery voice. "They are ready?"

Hamid the Hunchback nodded. "Three hundred of them wait your orders, *hazoor.*"

Maqboul smiled at his lieutenant. "What are you standing by that window like a nervous monkey for? Here is a night for love and comfort, you fool. I must have my prettiest wife from the harem beside me. Put down that silly club and bring me my zither and call little Nyura to my side."

Hamid the Hunchback dropped the lead club to the tiles and reached for the zither, thereby making the last move of his life.

A wild, savage figure dived from the rhododendrons outside the window, cleared the sill at a flying leap and landed with a crash on Hamid's hump. The Persian geni collapsed with a shriek. A fierce hand closed on the lead club, and the bludgeon smashed down on Hamid's head. Skull pulped to a turnip, Hamid sprawled on the rugs.

Maqboul el Mussulmanni bounced up off his cushions with a yowl of terror.

The little American curio-hunter caught the Turkoman with a flying tackle that hurled them both across the room in a cloud of carpets and kindling. A trap of steel fingers was closed on Maqboul's throat. Eyes like polished dagger-points burned into his bulging optics.

"My men!" he squalled in spasms of choked words. "They'll get you. My men—"

The white hand choked out the noise. Maqboul's eyes bulged like bird's eggs. His fists slammed on Peter Scarlet's face, and blood leaked into the curio-hunter's white beard. Kicking, biting, hyena-squeals issuing from his mouth, the Turkoman wrenched his shoulders free of the floor. With every last once of power left in him, Scarlet strove to drive home the club.

Locked together, Turkoman and curio-hunter rolled across the tiles. Maqboul el Mussulmanni had the advantage of unweakened strength. Peter Scarlet had only the club. Starved, nerves shredded by his battle for life in the tower and his fight for freedom with the rocking-stone, sick from drugs and horror and his haunted race across the valley, the curio-hunter had nothing save the fury of his heart to strengthen his hands. The Turkoman's fists belted Scarlet's face. Scarlet slugged with the club. Back and across the floor they wallowed, legs entwined, his beard tangled with the red whiskers of the other.

Maqboul got his teeth in Scarlet's wrist. The curio-hunter struck again and again, but in such close quarters he could scarcely wield his weapon. Blood trickled down his elbow. The Turkoman's teeth were clamped fast. Peter Scarlet's mind spun with pain.

With a cry of agony, the little American curio-hunter caught the Turkoman a blow on the chin with his butting head. Rugs slid, skidding against a wall, and an oil lamp fell, showering glass. Darkness plunged over the room, livened by the whistle of laboring lungs, moans and the dull slump of blows.

Had Hamid the Hunchback, nesting in his corner, been able to listen he would have heard a moaning, rattly and shrill, play weird harmony to a sodden, undertone groan. He would have heard the rattly, shrill moans come to a sudden, deathly stop.

Then, had Hamid the Hunchback been able to look, he might have been surprised to see a lone figure slip away from that tumbled room. A lone figure wearing a white robe and green turban. A squat, bulgy figure with a tousled crimson beard that blew as he ran, and an emerald thumb-ring that shimmered green fire on his hand.

MAJOR JOHN BURNT of the British Police leapt from his chair, hand snatching for the Webley on his belt; then stepped back with an astonished shout.

"Of all the— Well, I *am* damned. If it isn't old Scarlet! Peter Scarlet! Well, what the bloody fiend are you doing in that get-up—"

"Rather ghastly, eh?" The little American curio-hunter shuddered. He slumped into a chair and grabbed for the whisky decanter. A wry smile twisted his lips as he drank; then he turned on the officer, grimacing. "But I got him, Major. I got Maqboul and his right-hand man. Struck 'em dead with the same club they killed poor old Smith with. Right in his house I killed him. Had to pull a get-away. Valley strewn with his tribesmen. So I pulled on his duds and stuck on this emerald ring. You can have it. Wouldn't keep the thing for a million dollars, even if it did help me masquerade through those Moslem brigands.

"And this beard of mine. Whooey! Have to shave off the thing. His whiskers were red, you know, and I had to dye mine. You can guess what I used for dye. Yeh. He bit open my wrist and there was dye all over the place—"

Major John Burnt swore loudly, and the little American curio-hunter nodded. "That's right, Major. But he had me tied up in a Parsee burial tower tight as a drum, and the vultures were after me. You won't know how I got out of that. Poor old Smith got me out. The devils had put him away in that tower, see."

The little American curio-hunter's hand shook oddly as he thrust it under his cloak and drew to light a little disc of glass. He swallowed three noggins of whisky after he laid the little glass on the desk before the major.

It was a long time until Peter Scarlet could speak. "There it is," he whispered softly. "Smith's monocle. It—it was still in his eye. The sun was focused through it, Major. Like a burning glass. That ray would have set a plank on fire. As for rope—"

The major nodded slowly. Scarlet poured two long drinks. "To Smith!" The drinks were lifted high, and the glass disc on the desk winked and shone.

PETER SCARLET'S FUNERAL

ANOTHER ADVENTURE OF Peter Scarlet in this issue of *Action Stories*. The author of this well-known series, Theodore Roscoe, centers his story this time about one of the most unusual sect customs of the Far East. The following letter gives a brief view behind the scenes:

> Although I've spent a good deal of time in southern Asia, I still have to rely on my father for many of the intimate details of native customs. Had it not been for him, I probably never would have written "Towers of Silence." Of course, I might have guessed at the interior of the Parsee burial tower, written of it

as I figured it *should* be, and it might have gotten by. But I don't like to work that way.

How he got his information, I have promised not to say. A year or so ago I wrote up one of his experiences in the Far East without disguising it sufficiently—and got the devil from father. A man could spend years in the Orient without learning the truths of the native customs. I have squatted at the camel-drivers' fires beyond the Talar Hills and have not forgotten their tales; I claim as one of my closest friends the son of a Parsee priest in Bombay; I have split a good many bottles with a Legion adjutant from Djebel Druse, yarning all night. I have spent much time in the East; of the last five years, more than three have been devoted to travel. But a man doesn't learn the secrets of the Orient in a year, nor a decade.

The burial towers, forbidding structures with vultures hovering above, are scattered throughout the East wherever there is a Parsee settlement. In Bombay, where there is an especially large Parsee population, these towers stand in a beautiful garden on Malabar Hill. Each is about twenty-five feet high, built of stone, and has a small door at the side for the entrance of the body. In other places, where the sect is not so powerful, secret, underground entrances lead to the towers, and no visible entry breaks the solid stone of the walls.

As for the details, I refer you back to the story.

THEODORE ROSCOE

THE KILLER OF KELANTAN

*Several tons of enraged elephant make a risky
cargo at best; and hunter Bradshaw found
affairs at their worst aboard that freighter*

CHAPTER I

BRADSHAW'S ELEPHANT

THIS IS BRADSHAW'S incredible story, and it started over a plate of soup at dinner one night in Penang, when the tropic sun was rolling down the west like a blazing chariot wheel, and cool blue shadows were stealing around our veranda screens.

Bradshaw was the tall sunburned naturalist with the pepper-and-salt head of hair, the quiet smile and the china-blue eyes that had peeked into most of the nooks and crannies in Asia and the far East Indies. He'd collected everything from purple spiders to the rare albino rhinoceros of Nepal; and shipped more boat loads of animals across the seven seas than old man Noah ever dreamed of. A leathery, iron-nerved out-trailer Bradshaw was; and you wouldn't think anything like a dish of soup could have upset him.

But he sipped a spoonful, and on my word, you'd have thought he'd swallowed a dose of rat poison. His spoon clattered to the floor. His face went into a greenish knot. He dabbed at his lips with a napkin, coughing.

"I'm sick," he groaned, pushing back from the table. "Awful sick!"

He looked sick, too. Dampish on the forehead.

"But what the devil!" I cried in dismay. The soup had tasted all right to me. "What's wrong? Are you poisoned?" I'd seen Bradshaw eat Hindu candy many a time! "It's nothing but plain, old-fashioned ox-tail soup!"

"Ox-tail soup!" he sputtered. "Whoosh! Take it away!" He

Again and again he aimed the useless little weapon

made a face. "My word! I actually swallowed some of it! Soup manufactured from a tail!" He mopped his forehead, and turned to the young British consular agent who was our host. "Sorry," he apologized with a rueful smile. "But that's the one thing in the world I can't down. There's a story behind it, too. A mighty wild yarn. I'd better tell it."

"You better had!" we cried.

So out of that startling soup plate came a story of treachery and terrific battle, of murderous assault and savage plotting that ended with a .475 bullet going into somebody's head, a strange debauchery and a far stranger luncheon. All in all, one of the maddest adventures in Asia I ever heard. But judge for yourself. Here's the story.

DID YOU ever hear, Bradshaw began, of the Sanglerang River in that strip of sour Malay coast known as Kelantan? It's not a nice place. The jungle grows so fast that if you don't look out when the sun goes down the vines are liable to close in and strangle you. Hot, too. And where the river dumps out into the

Gulf of Siam it's so quiet and drugged you think you're at the edge of the world.

You are. The Gulf of Siam rolls away and away to nowhere beyond the sand bars. Once every five months the government boat puts into the delta for a look; and once in a blue moon a freighter tramps over the horizon.

It's a mighty lonely coast, and there are mosquitoes. Not the hit-and-run kind; but the kind that stay with you. The lazy black kind that sit down on your arm and shoot a hypodermic of poison into your veins.

I guess the good Lord stewed up the Sanglerang that day he didn't feel well. No honest white man would go there if he could help it. The only reason I was there was that I couldn't help it. I had to get that white elephant!

Peterboro, Ltd., of London, put me on the trail. "We want a white elephant," they demanded. "The best specimen you can bag. There's an Indian prince in the Punjab willing to pay anything for a white elephant. Get one for us and we'll top your usual price by two thousand pounds."

Well, I wasn't anxious for such a job, but I needed the money

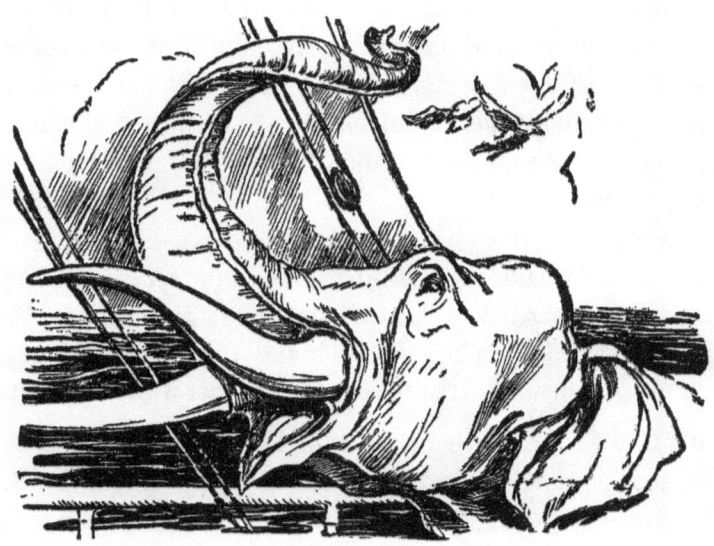

badly and knew just the elephant the Peterboro outfit wanted. The previous year I'd gone up the east Malay coast after climbing fish, and I'd heard about a jungle giant that had the natives climbing trees when its name was whispered.

It seemed this beast had ruled the Sanglerang territory for years, trampling around like a tornado and laughing at the native traps. Naturalists and collectors had gone after the creature, to come back empty-handed but open-mouthed. Taking the stories with the usual grain of salt and an extra shot of quinine, it was obvious that there was on the Sanglerang bottoms, an elephant of vast proportions and unusually white skin. White elephants aren't usually white, but sort of a light gray. But the natives on the coast claimed this elephant was white as sand, and their hunters wouldn't kill it because it was sort of sacred. It seemed, however, that old jumbo had assassinated plenty of them; gaining himself the name and reputation of a killer.

All right, I had just enough capital to get my boys and outfit together and hit for the Sanglerang after the famous killer. And when I flushed that tusker out of a Kelantan marsh one afternoon after weeks of tracking, I knew he wasn't notorious for nothing.

My boys shinned up the trees and I went up with them; and that elephant went by underneath like a hurricane in a tissue paper factory. He tore right under my *kaladang* roost, and he looked like the biggest animal in the world since prehistoric times. Man, he was a dandy! And when I saw his ivory I almost flopped out of the tree.

He was going like a storm, trunk raised, eyes a-shine, ears out like enormous fans, tusks lashing through the spear grass like mammoth sabers. Wow! he was the world's best elephant by far, and I yelled when he vanished in the vines. From then on I wanted nothing of life but the catching of that white elephant.

SOME DAY go out in a tempest and try to catch a chunk of chained lightning! That trick would be dead easy compared with the catching of that giant killer in that upper Malay backwater.

We trailed that devil for days. The days ran into weeks, and the weeks melded into two months.

We went ragged and sore. We went thin. I was a shivering, quinine-drugged wreck. The elephant became an obsession. I followed that Satan through forests and swamps and pestholes, through vines and clouds of mosquitoes and sunshine like a swat on the head. It was like following a cyclone—a cyclone that was liable to make a sudden about-face and abruptly follow you.

That's just what the old boy did. We chased him and he chased us and we chased him. And remember, it was no "dead or alive" proposition. I had to bring that demon jumbo back alive. I carried a .475 elephant gun to be used only in case the monster got his tusks into my ribs. I also carried a little .22 Webley that was just about right for those Sanglerang River mosquitoes. My boys carried chains and ropes and Malay flags to warn off jungle ghosts.

Maybe you think that big tusker was going to stand around and be trussed by chains and ropes and Malay flags to warn off ghosts. Not on your life! That big devil got going whenever we came near. He either moved away or moved at us, and when an elephant moves, he moves! He led us one dandy little dance in that steaming pest-hole, and toward the last I knew he was playing with us.

That made me mad. That old bull smelled out every trap I could devise, nibbled at the bait like a fish, laughed and went away. There I was chasing a will-o'-the-wisp piece of tunnage and dynamite, and half the time he didn't let me see him at all.

It drove me wild. I dreamed about that elephant, schemed about that elephant, lay awake plotting and biting my thumbs. I'd always considered myself a pretty fair trapper, and this white behemoth was knocking me around like a schoolboy. Talk about a chase! Don't forget, an elephant is smart as a scholar, can outrun a horse and beat up any creature in the jungle. And that killer was the smartest of them all.

"I'll get him," I said to myself, "if it's the last thing on God's earth I ever do." And finally I got him. Right on the delta of the Sanglerang that devil stumbled into an elephant pit we'd laid at the start of the race, and I had him fast. Or thought I did.

Wow! He was a beauty. After my boys got the ropes on him I took a good look and the hair really rose on my scalp. He was a monster. His tusks were good for all of a hundred and thirty pounds of ivory, worth well into a thousand dollars alone. His ears measured around seventeen feet from tip to tip. Maybe that will give you an idea.

And his spirit was immeasurable. Before we got him hog-tied he broke three chains, laid two of my boys out in lavender and walloped me across the arm with his trunk, neatly fracturing my left wrist. That bull was just so many tons of dynamite, believe me. He was just one quivering mountain, squealing and plunging and winking eyes wicked as a witch's curse. My heart pounded, though. He was the finest specimen of anything I'd ever captured, and he was worth a fortune. I felt like a painter who'd worked for years and just put the last daub on his masterpiece when I finally got the last chain on that bull.

BUT I hadn't counted on the old devil's influence. Now that I had him in bonds my Malay boys were looking greener than ever under the gills. The elephant made a savage rumpus that night, and in the morning every last one of my boys had lit out, taking most of the rations with them. Those cursed bearers were feeling guilty. They'd captured a sacred white elephant, but they couldn't face him afterward. How I cursed those Malays!

Well, there I was on the Sanglerang delta with my white elephant. I was literally in rags, shivering with malaria, empty-handed with my fortune, and a broken left wrist to boot. The dawn came up like a furnace blast and I sat down in the mud and slugged at mosquitoes and shot oaths up at the sky. I said the Sanglerang was world's end and no place for an honest white man.

A mile down the river there was a huddle of native huts, but the fishermen wouldn't come near me. In front of me was a logy, sluggish green river full of spawning, yawning croco-diles. Behind me was the worst neck of jungle in the East. And eastward the Gulf of Siam rolled off blue and still to a horizon empty as the Sahara.

Now, how was I going to get that red-eyed monster of an elephant out of there? You can't carry an elephant on your back, that's the truth. I'd counted on sending a runner down to Pech-aburi to locate a ship, and now there wasn't a single runner or anybody else to send. The village fishermen wouldn't go. They sneaked up for a look at my prize in the pit, then ran away squeaking like mice. They wouldn't help me. I fired six dialects at them and they slammed their wishbones in the mud and pretended not to understand.

By noon I was practically foaming at the mouth. I tramped the river bank in a blast-furnace heat, sweating and shiver-ing with a swell dose of malaria, a perfect picture of the man stranded with a million dollars on a desert isle. A ship? There wouldn't be one for five months, when the government packet put in. The horizon was just a streak of vacant blue. I tell you, no honest white man would put into the Sanglerang if he could help it.

That's why I yelled like a fool when I did see a smoke-smudge steaming down the horizon. And when that bull-nosed seven-seas tramp, the Lily of Falmouth, heaved over the rim and plod-ded straight into the soupy Sanglerang to drop her hook not twenty feet offshore that afternoon I thought Allah and Buddha were working like sixty for my side.

The Lily of Falmouth was squat and dirty, with red lead smudged on her rakish hull, an umbrella of smoke dropping millions of cinders on her unpainted decks, and soiled garments and garbage and deck-gear strewn along her rails. But she looked more beautiful to me than Morgan's yacht. And when her skip-per came ashore to answer my hail I thought the world was a great place after all.

Coppard, he said his name was. Cap'n Coppard. He was

angular and lean-muscled in a suit of dirty whites, and the thumbs were missing from both hands, and his gaunt long face was freckled with great yellow liver spots. The missing thumb gave me a creep when he shook hands, but I was in no mood to criticize the lack of thumbs and the bad liver of anybody who would bring a ship into the Sanglerang just then.

Besides, Captain Coppard was blessed with a great shock of snowy hair, very benevolent, and friendly blue eyes set in crinkly, humorous wrinkles; and his voice was genial.

"You want to ship an elephant? Sure you can. Got the whole jolly fore-deck for him. Get him aboard easy with a sling and them deck booms. Plenty o' room. I'm travelin' light an' just put in to fix a rudder post. We'll git your bull aboard an' be outa here by tomorrow mornin'."

Those words were music to my buzzing ears, let me tell you. The captain took me aboard for a swizzle and then followed me ashore to have a look at my prize. He whistled through his teeth when he saw that elephant, and chuckled, running his four fingers through his mop of white hair.

"Say, she's a beauty of a bull, all righto! I'll send my crew along to hoist her." He turned his mild blue eyes on me. "You're lucky, Mr. Bradshaw. There wouldn't be no other boat in here for a long time." When he smiled the liver blotches on his face took on a bluish tinge. "No, sir!" he repeated. "There won't be no other craft over that horizon for a good long time."

I clapped my hand on my cheek and killed seven mosquitoes. I agreed with Captain Coppard that I was very lucky indeed. Let me pronounce here and now that I agreed with Captain Coppard entirely too soon.

CHAPTER II

UP IN A TREE

WE GOT THE giant killer aboard the Lily of Falmouth only by the grace of Heaven and that ancient Greek scientist who invented the block tackle and the lever. Certainly the native fishermen didn't help us. They wouldn't come near that sacred elephant for all the gin and curses we could hand them. Captain Coppard got his deck crew ashore, and then his engine room gang.

This deck crew and black gang were about the toughest-looking crowd of Dutch sea-wallopers I'd ever seen, and the two Dutch mates looked like buccaneers from a pirate galleon. But they edged their ship around in the deep channel, rigged up enough ropes to lift the Woolworth Building, and hoisted the elephant high and dry to the steamer's broad fore-deck. The skipper relayed my instructions to the crew in Dutch.

That devil elephant assisted our efforts not at all. He broke a chain, stepped on the second mate's foot, smashed in a sailor's nose with his whipping trunk, and dug out a section of rail with his tusk before he was through. When he felt the deck booms hoisting him skyward he let out a blast that almost blew us out of the river. Tons of fighting, kicking, biting wild animal dropped to the fore-deck and shivered the ship, and it was dawn before we had him fast.

I thanked Heaven for the Lily of Falmouth when she stood out to sea at last. She might have been made for the requirements of shipping that big, brute, white elephant. Her bow was stout and wide with plenty of deck space. The winches were well up on the fore-peak. Anchor engines and all that sort of thing. Then the foremast was set well forward, and there was broad deck back to the bridge.

Stowed directly in front of the bridge were a number of iron barrels, oil containers. Atop these barrels sat a row of red wooden hogsheads. This made sort of a wall that would shadow the open deck.

I had the crew go ashore to cut several bales of swamp grass and foliage, enough to keep the monster alive till we reached civilization; and this stuff was piled on the bow.

Then the raving elephant was slung to the deck aft of the foremast and tied by about thirty stout hawsers in a standing position. The ropes ran in every direction, attaching the beast to each rail, to deck-bitts, to wheel chucks, to the mast, and to the lowered booms. When it was over, the big behemoth could move his feet about two inches. His tusks were caught by nooses. He had a little leeway to swing his trunk and flap his ears, but that was about all. By George, he looked like a monstrous spider in the center of some queer manner of web! He fairly shook with fury.

"You won't get out of there, old boy," I promised him. And I laughed when he glared at me with his wicked little red eyes. He hated me. You bet he did! He knew I was responsible for his plight, and he didn't take those bloodshot eyes off me for a second.

"He's dangerous, that fellow," Captain Coppard observed, looking down from the bridge. "Biggest tusker I ever see. Pretty swell ivory, eh?" The captain chuckled and appraised. It seemed he had handled elephants before.

He helped me rig up a water tank, a big iron trough about three feet deep which he moored under the wall of oil containers and hogsheads. He helped me in a thousand other ways. Captain Coppard, I said to myself, was a gentleman.

The Lily of Falmouth stood out to sea, her engines hammering, her funnel spouting smoke, and I went to Coppard's cabin sighing with relief. He offered me a bunk and said I could stow my duffle in with his. That was mighty decent of him. The cabin was shabby, but blessed with screens, and the captain was free at passing around his refreshments.

After a good whisky peg I went out on deck and gloated at the horrible shore I was leaving behind. Everything was going beautifully. The sea was like glass; hot, smooth glass. The only ripple was made by a pair of shark-fins cutting water off the beam like tiny sailboats.

"Yeah!" Captain Coppard said at my elbow. "Water's full of sharks off here. Hundreds of 'em. No place for a swim, eh?"

No place for a swim, all right. The sharks began to come from all directions. They crisscrossed under our bow and cruised under our churning stern.

The captain grinned. "Wildest bit of coast along here I ever saw. It's way off the sea lane. It would be tough to get stuck out here. The channel's treacherous. But we won't get stuck. I never run so light in all my life. That there elephant's the first cargo I've had up from Singapore. I reckon we ain't overloaded."

QUEER HOW it happened. We must have been three miles out by that time, thumping down the hottest, stillest desert of water ever sailed. One of the Dutch mates had just clanged four bells on the upper bridge; and the captain had started to tell me about a storm that had removed all but one lifeboat—"that there one on the stern"—when there was a grinding bump under the bows and the Lily of Falmouth came to a dead stop.

The jar almost knocked me to my face, and I rushed down to the fore-deck for a look at my precious elephant. Coppard began to yell, and his voice brought sailors running. He sent them aft for some reason, and came down to the fore-deck cursing.

"Damn it, Mr. Bradshaw, we're on a bar!"

The engines went silent, and a big fog of black smoke piled down out of the funnel, choking the decks. The big bull let a blast out of his trunk, and I mopped my face.

"Aground?"

The skipper ran his thumbless hand through his white mop and nodded unhappily.

"Looks like it. These waters ain't charted in here. I reckon that bull o' yours is heavier than he looks. Say!" The captain pointed aloft in the sunshine. "Just run up there to the crow's-nest an' see if you can sight shoal water off to starboard, will you? I'm gonna drop a lead-line off the bow. Call down an' tell me if you see green water off there."

The captain picked up an ax one of the sailors had left at the foot of the bridge ladder, carefully skirted the elephant, and went to the bow. Anxious to be of service, I ducked around the trussed jungle giant and made for the foremast. I wasn't a sailor, but I knew the crow's-nest was that little box high up the mast where the lookout stood watch.

It didn't occur to me to wonder why a sailor hadn't been up there from the start. Obediently I climbed up the steep ladder, clinging for dear life to the iron rungs, and pulling myself into the crow's-nest with all the nervousness of a steeple jack on his first chimney. It was high up there in that little box. I looked for green water to starboard, and saw a lot of it. I also saw a lot of sharks bellying around in the depths of it. The sun reflected off the water in a blinding blaze; and I cursed the skipper under my breath for running us aground just when we had such a good start.

The skipper yelled something up at me. He was standing at the winch on the fore-peak, and suddenly the winch began to clatter; there was a cloud of red dust and a splash under the bow. For some reason the anchor chain had let go.

"Stay up there," the captain shouted through cupped hands, "an' tell me how the water looks off to port."

I looked off to port. The next minute I heard a wild squeal come up to the sky from my elephant. The devil! Listen! You'll never guess what I saw when I glared down the length of that confounded mast. I glared down that mast and, as I live and exhale, if Captain Coppard of the thumbless hands, white hair and liver-spotted face wasn't scurrying around that elephant with his ax flashing silver light in the sunshine.

I screamed. The elephant bellowed. Captain Coppard went right ahead; he brought down his ax and cut one rope after another, *chop, chop, chop!*

"COPPARD!" I shrieked down at him. I was half out of the crow's-nest by that time, one kicking leg trying to find the ladder rung. "What are you doing?"

He knew what he was doing, all right. He chopped the ropes from the fore legs of that giant elephant, slashed the hawsers strung to the deck booms, dodged the giant's lashing trunk and smashed the chain that moored his belly to a wheel chuck.

If that elephant didn't have a Roman holiday, then! He reared up like exploding dynamite, trumpeting, kicking his forefeet and stabbing with his tusks and hurling his bulk from side to side so that the ship shook from stern to stem. But that captain hadn't cut all the ropes, no sir! He'd cut just enough to hold the elephant till he could streak up the narrow bridge ladder; and then when he got to the bridge he brought down his ax on the two main hawsers that had been strung from the elephant's rear legs to the bridge wings.

Wow! I hung out of the crow's-nest high on that foremast, paralyzed and pop-eyed, unable to move a hand. The elephant was now heaving like fury on the few remaining ropes, and would break free any second.

Safe on the bridge deck, Captain Coppard was waving his ax and yelling. The words trickled like green knives into my ears above the shrieking of the white elephant; hung me, panting, on that high perch, weak as if my neck was broken.

"He's mine!" that Captain Coppard was yelling. "He's all mine, Mr. Bradshaw. Nicest bit of elephant I ever seen. Worth a tidy fortune. No hard feelin's, you unnerstand. Just a bit o' business. The ship's grounded, see, an' anchored, too. I'm goin' ashore fer help, that's all. I'm takin' all the crew an' all the food, an' I'm awful sorry I can't take you, but it's impossible to save you since the tusker's broke free, see?"

The sweat burst out like icicles from my pores.

"What the devil do you mean?" I screamed.

"Me an' my men is leavin'," Coppard chanted cheerfully. "We're goin' ashore with the lifeboat, an' then we're goin' by land up to Pechaburi. When we gets there we hires a gov'ment launch to bring us back. We'll be back in just about two weeks with the gov'ment man. We got all the food, Mr. Bradshaw. You can't live without it, but the elephant will survive fine. Elephant won't mind the heat like you will, neither. It'll be right tuckered when we get back, but you'll be dead."

I was cawing like a crow. Cawing curses and scarlet oaths. Waving my bad left wrist.

"Murderer!" I squalled. "Hey! Sailors! Help!"

"Sailors are all aft," Coppard shouted. Turning, he bawled at some men behind the bridge. One of the Dutch mates came forward; stared pop-eyed at me and the elephant. Coppard yelled Dutch at him, and he raised his hands in what I took to be horror, and fled aft again. I screamed at that mate for help, but he disappeared. Coppard just laughed.

"They don't know English," he said. "I just told 'em you were crazy. I told 'em you were a madman an' you insisted on stayin' with your elephant an' wouldn't come down. I told 'em you were a dangerous maniac, an' there ain't nothin' to do but leave you here while we go for help. They're scairt stiff o' you!"

I MUST have looked like a maniac, that's the truth. I'd have given my right eye for a Dutch vocabulary just then. My left eye, too. Those confounded Hollander seamen. They hadn't seen their lovely skipper free the tusker. He'd told them I was insane. It would make a nice story for the government agent. I could just hear Captain Coppard saying:

"We hated to leave him, but what could we do? He was 'way up the mast and would have killed the first guy who come near. We maybe coulda shot the bull to get him, but I didn't dare risk my men—" Sweet Captain Coppard! The government man would believe it, too. Men do go insane in the tropics.

"Murderer!" I bawled. "If I ever get out of here, I'll—"

"The elephant will see you don't come down," the benevolent ship's master explained. "There won't be no ships come near to let you down, neither. And the native fishermen, even if they did hear you holler, wouldn't come near you 'count of the sacred elephant. You might try leapin' off the mast an' swimmin' to shore, but the sharks ain't friendly. I guess maybe you'll just dive offa there into the water anyhow, when the sun comes up hot day after to-morrow, an' you're gettin' hungry. You see—"

Now I could hear a great to-do somewhere around the stern, and I guessed the Dutch sea dogs were lowering away.

"Murderer!" I shrieked.

"Aw, no," the genial mariner called. "I ain't killin' you, am I? I'd just as soon put a bullet in you or give you a belayin' pin or the deep six, but then one o' my crew woulda seen it an' snitched some time. Now they all see me leavin' you here alive, an' they think I'm runnin' to get help for you. The police will say I did just right. I'll show 'em how it was the elephant you cut loose before you run up the mast. I'll show 'em how the ship's run aground, an' they won't criticize me for leavin' it an' a ravin' maniac aboard it, too.

"Two weeks from now you'll be croaked, but they'll know it's the tusker who done it. There ain't no bullets or stool pigeons to point at me. The gov'ment man will help me get clear o' the shoals, an' I reckon he'll buy the elephant, too. I'm sorry, Mr. Bradshaw," Captain Coppard called sympathetically, "but I ain't had a cargo in a long time, an' I need the gold that there bull will bring. Reckon I'll get a neat price for him when I fat him up after his two weeks bant."

Well, that mean, white-headed, criminal-faced, yellow-livered, scum-souled master of the Lily of Falmouth! He smirked up at me from his stance on the bridge, and doffed his dirty sea cap.

"Well, g'by, Mr. Bradshaw."

"Good-by, Mr. Bradshaw" was right! I had got out of the crow's-nest by that time, and halfway down the tapering iron ladder. And by that time, also, the raging tons of bull elephant on the fore-deck under me broke completely free. That bull put down his cement head and closed his eyes and hurled himself forward and hit the base of the mast a battering-ram smash that almost rang me off the rungs!

I hope to die if I didn't yell like a steam siren. I got an elbow through one rung, pushed back my sun helmet, snatched for my belt and yanked into action that little .22 Webley pistol. A bullet in the face was just the thing for that smiling pirate on the bridge; and I let fly a crackling salvo.

But the genial Captain Coppard ducked the shot, waved a gaunt hand, and fled behind a stanchion. The elephant hit the mast under me again; and I hung on the ladder howling like a fool.

I didn't hear the lifeboat being lowered aft, but a moment later I saw the confounded craft bobbing off astern. Captain Coppard and his two Dutch buccaneers and his crew of sea-wallopers were stuffed in that boat, and so was a crate of food. I fired five hundred oaths at the craft and two bullets. But the little .22 pistol should have been a cannon; and the bullets only kicked up little founts of froth at the halfway mark where cool shark fins cut the glassy, steel-hued water.

At the base of the mast on which I hung, the giant white bull elephant was running a furious merry-go-round; eyes blazing like fanned coals, tusks shining sharp and white, bits of rope and lengths of chain flying and jangling from his trampling feet, his trunk lifted high and trumpeting like a thousand bugles in a victorious Roman legion!

CHAPTER III

ROASTED ALIVE

GET THIS PICTURE. A rusty, sea-bitten old tramp freighter lolling on a sand bar three miles off the Malay coast far up the Gulf of Siam. The Gulf of Siam rolling away and away to nowhere, blue and hot and still as glass under a savage brass sun. The distant coast a green strip under the furnace sky, a shimmering green strip that marks the mouth of a river where no honest man would go—and when a lifeboat stuffed with men vanishes from view in that river mouth it only proves the statement.

That coast is far away. The tramp freighter is lost on a vacant, vast desert of lonely water and lonely sky.

The sun makes shimmering heat waves dance on the freighter's iron plates. It comes down from the sky like a bath of fire, and slants up off the mirroring water like lances of white flame. The stranded ship bakes.

Sharks glide and ripple and cut the metal water under the ship's bow and stern. Those silent, crisscrossing fins! Hungry sharks. But they're going to stay hungry, because there isn't any garbage coming over the rail. That's because there's no fire in the freighter's galley and no food in the lazaret. The cook has gone.

So have the captain and the crew. The funnel has even grown tired of smoking, after petering out on the job and leaving a rain of cinders powdering the decks. The cabins are empty, the wheelhouse is vacant, the bridge is deserted.

But directly under the vacant bridge the deck is piled with a wall of iron oil containers, and a row of big red barrels that top the iron cans. On the fore-deck in front of those cans and barrels there is a sign of life. Several tons of it that get madder and madder and hotter and hotter and hungrier and wilder with every inch the red-hot sun takes across the brass sky.

The elephant tramples around in circles. Rushes to the tank under the row of hogsheads to get a drink. Thunders up the bow for a snatch at some exceedingly dry grass. Charges back to butt the foremast a terrific smash with its lowered head. Then it winds its trunk around the foremast, sharpens its tusks on the foremast or just stands glaring up the mast with wicked red eyes.

There's another piece of life hanging around, too. It hangs 'way up the foremast in the lookout nest. It's not a monkey, but it certainly isn't a man, though it seems to be wearing a sun helmet and some clothes. Its face is burned to a piece of raw steak, and it makes odd noises in its skinny throat. All in all, it doesn't seem worth much, but it fascinates the elephant stamping the deck far below.

The thing up the mast watches the elephant, then shakes its burned face, rubs its burned eyes, sticks out a swollen tongue and caws like a raven. There's no food up in that crow's-nest. No water. And not an iota of shade. He hollers, then yanks out a little .22 pistol and yells some more.

That .22 isn't much good. The thing in the crow's-nest might shoot it at the elephant below—and watch the bullets bounce off the elephant's white hide like peas off a cement wall. It weeps and groans and claws its unshaved jaw.

Listen, brother! Hunger and thirst are terrible affairs. I know. That thing up there in the crow's-nest was me!

I HAD to bite my lower lip and pinch my arms to keep from going to shreds right at the start. The first hour, watching that lifeboat dim out in the direction of the coast, was bad. I could see the sunshine flashing on the oars, and I cursed for every stroke.

When the lifeboat finally disappeared I slumped down in the bottom of the crow's-nest and felt mighty sick at the stomach. The sweat bubbled out on my face in great big beads of ice.

When I thought of Captain Coppard the nails drew blood in my clenched palms. The fiend must have plotted the whole affair the second he saw the giant tusker. He knew the value of elephants. He knew he could run the ship aground and stick me up the mast. I couldn't get down. The elephant would tramp me into pudding. I couldn't shoot the elephant with a .22. I couldn't dive off the mast and swim ashore because of the sharks. The sun would drive me mad. The thirst would make me insane. The hunger would starve me to death.

If I made a desperate rush to the elephant's water tank, the bull would get me. If it was only a question of a dash for cover I might have a chance. But I had to climb down a thin ladder on a thin mast. The bull could see my every move.

"I won't die!" I shouted to myself. "I won't!"

I looked down out of the crow's-nest. The elephant saw me and gave the mast a crack with his skull. Then he put his forefeet up on the ladder, reared up on hind legs and ran his trunk up the ladder rungs. I could see his fierce eyes burning like rubies. I fiddled with the Webley pistol; loaded the magazine. Six shots left. I couldn't kill that elephant with six hundred.

The sun flamed down the sky and vanished in the west, and a lot of stars came out behind a yellow moon. My lips began to dry out. I heard the elephant drinking, and the sound made my mouth ache.

Just for exercise I took a couple of silent steps down the ladder. That elephant heard me. He spun from the trough and came booming back to the mast, rubbing his massive flank against the mast-ladder. The mast trembled, and I got back into the nest.

I tried the same trick three times that night, and each time the devil heard my first move. Elephants sleep standing up. If I moved a finger up there his ears stood out like fans.

TOWARD MORNING I guess I slept, for I came to with a devil of a raw face, and the sunshine baking my eyes. And then I was thirsty. My tongue felt like a piece of smoked ham.

Let's not talk about the way it felt two days later, nor the way I hid my face with my coat and hunched my shoulders under the sun helmet, while noontime blasted down a blinding fire. Nor about the pain in my legs and back, the dull throb in my arms, the punching in my dry stomach.

Nor the way I glared off to sea and toward that sizzling, dim-distant ribbon of green shore line, first praying, then cursing for a boat. Nor the way I tried to sneak down the ladder and the elephant laid open the calf of my leg with a blow from his trunk.

Anyway, two days had flamed by and I was still alive. In that terrific tropic sunshine that was something!

The tropic sun blazed up out of the east to start the third twenty-four-hour drag, and I got pretty savage that day. My belt was down to the last notch and my eyes were simmering in my head. I got to looking at the shark-fins cutting the bright water, at the elephant galumphing around below; then at my pistol. That scared me. Maybe I'd go stark mad and pump a .22 into my head.

"I'll climb down the ladder and slam these beans into that elephant's right eye," I cursed. "I'll show him who's the killer!"

I climbed down the ladder. The second I hung out of the crow's-nest the elephant made a rush. Then he waited for me to come down, and I got to within three feet of his lashing trunk. There was the elephant's water tank, under the shadow of that wall of barrels. The water was half gone. It looked cool.

"Get back!" I screamed at the elephant.

I cursed, begged, threatened. I told myself I was going to shoot and make a dash for that water tank.

But I couldn't shoot. I didn't want to ruin my masterpiece. Weeping dusty tears, I climbed aloft and fell asleep.

While I was unconscious an afternoon blow came up, and it rained. I caught an inch of water in my sun helmet, and drank. Just enough to torture me and keep me alive. I learned how to suck water out of my soaked sleeve and wring it out of my leather boots, drop by drop. Then the sun blazed out hotter than ever.

GOD KNOWS what kept me going the fourth day. The agony in my starved stomach. The dust in my mouth. That terrible, blinding sun. I clambered down the mast and booed and shooed at the elephant. I fired the gun in the air to frighten him and he squealed in amusement. I crawled down to within three inches of his grabbing trunk and tried to kick the little feeler at the end of the snout. His red eyes twinkled and he flirted his tail.

I took off my jacket and hurled it at the bow, hoping the devil would make a dash after it and give me a chance to rush the water tank. The killer made a thundering lunge at the jacket; I scrabbled down the ladder; he whirled and came back like an express train; and I yanked myself up the mast just in time to keep from being smashed to pulp.

That old sweetheart down there was having a grand game. He'd finished off his dried provender, but he still had several buckets of water in the tank. He didn't mind the heat and the pangs of hunger were only making him more ugly and alert.

All that fourth afternoon he leaned against the mast, rubbing his flank against the ladder. I sat up in the crow's-nest with my tongue swelling out of cracked lips, too weak to move. One drink in four days.

Try looking at a tank of fast-vanishing water and listening to a behemoth sop up good cool snoutfuls while you bite the blood out of your caked lips. Then try playing Pop Goes the Weasel, shinning up and down the pole with a mad killer elephant dancing around underneath. Man, it's tough going!

That night I was just one jump ahead of yowling insanity. I remember playing little tricks on myself. Hiding the gun in one pocket, then in the other. Chewing the rims of my leather boots. Licking the dew off the iron rail of the lookout box. Falling asleep and waking up shrieking with the *blub-blub-blub* of a drinking elephant in my shriveled ears.

FINALLY, ON the fifth day of torture, only two things were keeping me alive. First was the hatred for Captain Coppard that burned like a little white coal in the back of my head;, which kept telling me what I'd do to him if I ever escaped. Second was the desire to get the best of that elephant.

All right. It didn't work that afternoon. That night I was dying of thirst and starvation. I was shrunk to a mummy, shivering in rags, panting with exhaustion, and dry as a leaf in a furnace. And when those Sanglerang River mosquitoes came out in a cloud to eat me, I was just about cooked and done.

Maybe you think mosquitoes won't hit you three miles out from shore. They can't smell you out there, eh? Those Sanglerang mosquitoes smelled me baking out there on that accursed ship, and they tame out in swarms for a Thanksgiving dinner. Those lazy, droning curs! They ate me alive. I had a nice little tussle with them up there, and they won. Elephant or no, I was going down!

I must have been a sight, a bloody, shivering, ragged mummy climbing, trembly and cursing out of that lookout box bathed in tropic moonlight, tongue jutting from my burned and weltered face.

Well, the tears rolled out of my eyes like pearls of molten brass as I struggled down that mast-ladder. I was doing just what that devil Coppard knew I'd do. I was going down to that elephant's water tank.

IN THE moonlight I went down, a broken, blattering, fried scarecrow with a fractured wrist and a ripped leg. The mosquitoes crawled across my face and tongue and eyes, stabbed me in the back, coiled and wreathed around me like brown smoke. I got my starved carcass down three more rungs. I was ghastly weak. Sick. I remember how I was crying. I was in terrible shape.

The giant white killer was standing at the foot of the mast with his trunk swinging, his eyes twinkling like brilliant rubies, his ears out like mammoth gray butterflies poised on either side of his monstrous head, his tail sticking straight up in the air. The moonshine polished his tusks till they glistened—a pair of terrible ivory swords. Soapy lather dribbled from his quivering lip. He began to swing his tons of body, rolling from side to side on his great, bunchy feet. He didn't make a sound.

The sharks out in the moonshine water knew something was doing. I could see the cruising fins, the pale white bellies leaning over in the bottle-green ripples. The brass tears coasted out of my eyes.

Bathed with mosquitoes, I clawed my way down the narrow ladder, straight for the elephant's ruby eyes. He shot his trunk snaking up at me, and rolled his shoulders with impatience. My hand on the gun was shaking like a withered twig. I got to within a foot of that python-like trunk. And then, so help me! I had to keep my nerve up by looking at the water tank. I hadn't looked at that elephant's drinking trough for the past five hours. I'd been saving it to give me the added punch I was going to need for the end.

When I got down that ladder, breathed hard and took a look, I got it square between the eyes. The elephant had been thirsty, too. That tank was dry as a bone!

That was the last straw! I shrieked out a laugh, and swung my gun. *Slam!* I fired at that elephant, but I couldn't have hit the broad side of a mountain. The .22 spat in the moonlight; the bullet whizzed over the bull's rearing head and struck somewhere with a *bing!*

Then I saw it had streaked across the deck and plunked into one of those big red hogsheads that sat in a row atop the wall of oil containers behind the elephant's trough.

And what do you think happened then? Why, a little hole appeared in that big red barrel, and a spout of white liquid came out through the hole. I hung on the ladder and glared with burning eyes. Talk about torture! The sight of that white stream spouting from the barrel and arching through the moonbeams and hitting the bottom of the elephant's trough with a musical splash was torture for me. The stream glistened and I clawed my paper lips. The elephant snorted. The mosquitoes droned like airplanes.

The liquid arched down into the elephant's tank from that red barrel I'd punctured, and suddenly I was yelling like a fool. I could smell it! The breeze came along and gave me a whiff. I turned my shaking pistol on those barrels sitting above the elephant's trough, and I let fly. *Slam! Slam! Slam!* Five bullets I had; and I knocked five holes in the bottom of five of those red barrels, and five streams of silver spouted down into the elephant's open tank.

My pistol was empty now, but my brain was stuffed full and whizzing like a chariot in a race. Talk about the laughing rill of the brook, the chant of the tide in the sea—mere Tin Pan Alley jazz compared to the symphony of those punctured barrels, the splash of silver liquid falling into that elephant's tank.

You can bet the elephant listened, too. He must have been pretty dry. He took his red eyes off me for a second and watched the filling tank, ears fanning. It made me laugh. I laughed all the way back up that mast. I laughed when I got back into the crow's-nest. I huddled down into that box, and smashed mosquitoes, and let all sorts of queer noises come out of my teeth.

A little while later I saw that the barrels had run dry and the tank was full. The elephant's snout was nosing into that sweet trough.

ANOTHER HALF hour and the old devil had emptied that whole tank. The trough was as dry as a burned-out furnace.

I forgot the mosquitoes. I forgot everything except thirst. Those red barrels! Five days I'd been up there—on one drink! My tongue was hanging out a foot, but I waited.

The clock was slow on the Gulf of Siam that night. The moon went down and the stars traveled slowly across a sky like painted cloth. The elephant down there looked like painted cloth, too.

I couldn't stand it any longer. I started down.

The tusker didn't move when I climbed from the crow's-nest this time. He didn't see me. His eyes were closed. I laughed so hard I almost fell off the ladder. I laughed at the sharks sneaking around beyond the rail and I laughed when I thought of Captain Coppard flinging up his thumbless hands in terror and surprise. And all the time I had my eyes on that row of red barrels.

But I laughed a little too soon. Just as I gained the fifth rung from the bottom of the mast-ladder the elephant gave a snort, reared and crashed out with his trunk. That giant trunk slapped me across the shoulders, and dropped me to the deck like a swatted fly.

Swock! I went rolling across the deck like a dummy, and the mammoth was after me. His trunk caught my legs and lifted me high in the air. The trunk let go, and I sailed. Twisting and turning I sailed up over a deck boom, and dropped with a smash on the anchor winch up in the bow.

I hit screaming on my jaw, square in a tangle of scrap iron and wheels. That fall sprained an ankle for me, dislocated my left shoulder, drove an iron cog into my stomach and broke open my face. I don't know why I wasn't killed. I guess there wasn't much of me to fall on that winch, and I just floated down like an empty bag.

Somehow I was still clutching the gun. The elephant came down on me, a thundering, booming avalanche. I hurled the gun and missed him by a mile. That was because the gun only went three feet in a lazy arc. I shrieked and kicked myself out of that winch and tried to run.

Crack! The elephant's trunk walloped my neck, and I went spinning down the deck like a collapsing toy.

The trunk had me again. I punched with fists of cotton. I was kicking high in the air, beating at the elephant's ears. I fought that elephant. He was crushing me alive. I could feel my ribs snapping like reeds. The breath went out of me in a gust. The world went red and black. I dropped to the deck ten feet away, and couldn't get up. I lay on my side and watched that giant tusker start toward me.

His shoulders rolled and he moved one mammoth foot. Then he moved the other. Slowly, slowly he came on. His trunk was swinging like the hand of a blind man. I tried to shriek, tried to scramble out of the way. I couldn't move an inch.

The elephant advanced like a slow-motion film. He was only five feet away. That bull was breathing hard. His trunk came out heavy as lead. I could feel it trying to grab my throat.

But he never grabbed. He dropped in a tired sort of way. The elephant's absurd front legs were buckling at the knees. His eyes were drowsy and flickering. He groaned. He settled to the deck on sinking legs. There was a thundering crash as he rolled on his side.

And then the biggest white elephant in the world was flat on the deck of the Lily of Falmouth, snoring like a blacksmith's bellows, out colder than Firpo!

BRADSHAW, THE tall naturalist from Kelantan, sighed up out of his chair and went to the veranda rail, mopping sweat from his leathery face. When he turned around again he was smiling.

"Well, that's about all," he said softly. "Nine days later the government boat cruised out of the Sanglerang. Captain Coppard was standing in the bow, running his thumbless hands through his benevolent white hair, and stretching a smile across his liver-spotted face. I was safe and somewhat alive up in the wheel house of the Lily of Falmouth, and ready to greet him.

"You see, I didn't die of thirst. When Jumbo keeled over I managed to move. I was so weak I had to crawl on my belly around the elephant, but I wasn't too weak to find the skipper's ax up on the bridge, and smash open one of those red barrels. Did I get a drink? Wow! I got enough to lift me up the companion ladder to the bridge, where I found my .475 elephant gun in the captain's cabin.

"I got enough to last me nine days so I could pull the trigger of that .475 cannon.

"Captain Coppard saw me moving around up on the bridge. I guess he lost his temper, or decided the show was over for him. The next thing I knew, bullets were zinging around me, and Coppard was sighting at me along his rifle.

"I was white-hot with anger at that. I raised the elephant gun and pulled that trigger like I never pulled a trigger before. What was left of the captain went flying out of the launch, and the sharks had him before you could say 'Jack Spratt.'"

Bradshaw sponged his face, and raised his glass through the silence.

"Here," he toasted, "is to a row of red barrels!"

"But what," panted the British consulate agent, "was in them?"

"Gin," said Bradshaw softly. "A few hundred gallons of warm gin!"

It was quiet on the veranda. The moon was nesting in a low cruising cloud and the indigo bay was restless under slow, bright stars.

"But, my heavens!" The British consulate attaché was sweating in his chair. "You were starving after that fifth day. And you were out there nine days more? How in the name of heaven— You said that captain took all the food off the boat! You couldn't have kept alive on gin. Why, if you hadn't eaten you'd have died."

"That's a fact," Bradshaw nodded, "so I ate. I got enough to keep me alive those last nine days. I hated to do it, I swear; but I crawled down to the fore-deck where that drunken elephant was still snoring, and I took the skipper's ax with me. It broke my heart to do it. But it didn't hurt him at all when the ax came down. And that's what I lived on.

"I got my price for that big white bull elephant, too. I delivered him safe and alive. He wasn't quite a perfect specimen, but you'd never notice unless you looked close, and Peterboro, Ltd., told their customer that the poor devil was born that way."

"But what," squawked the sweating Britisher, "did you eat?"

The naturalist mopped his face. "I had it three times a day and every day for nine days, and since then I haven't been able to face anything at all that remotely resembled it. Nine days without any side dishes. Think of it! For nine days," Bradshaw groaned, "I lived on that elephant's tail."

THE EMPEROR OF DOOM

Opals were the bait—gleaming eggs as black as sin,
worth the blood of a thousand South Sea cutthroats.
Peter Scarlet had them—but the cleverest thief
East of Suez swore they'd dangle from his turban.

A TONGUE OF vermilion light spouted from behind the breadfruit tree. A bullet tore up the balcony and whipped through the rattan blind with a gust of splinters. Peter Scarlet, the little American curio-hunter, danced up out of his chair and away from the window, a smoking rent in his cuff. A fuzzy white ball of smoke drifted up in the moonlight; and by the time the startled curio-hunter got himself out of the hotel and charged, gun in hand, down the street even the smoke was gone.

It had been close. Back in his hot room Scarlet eyed the tear in his sleeve. "H'mmmm." He looked at the hole in the window blind. "Ha." He chuckled. His assailant wasn't so smart, perhaps. After all, a fellow who shot at a shadow on a blind and failed to figure in the angle of deflection wasn't the brightest gunman in the world.

But a pearl of sweat leaked down the little American's leathery cheek just the same. In the street below his balcony there were voices. Other folk who had heard the shot. Well, they wouldn't find the sharpshooter now. The chap had worked a quick and masterful getaway.

Somewhere down by the waterfront an old clock chimed three. Peter Scarlet crossed his room, opened his battered kitbag and drew out a crumpled letter. He read the letter, smiled in spite of it, chucked it into his pocket, then turned out the moth-pestered oil lamp. With his Lüger automatic in his fingers, he sidled up to the window once more, and peeked through the rattan blind. The street below was deserted to shadows. Beyond were tin and wooden roofs backed by a fringe of palms. Beyond the palms lay the dark bay. A skinny funnel was lifted above a clutter of sampan masts. That was the coastal steamer lolling at anchor. The funnel smoked in the moonlight.

"She'll be off for Java," Scarlet said, pocketing his gun. Then he grinned. In the room next to his a man was snoring, and the sound came through the thin wall like the echo of a motor. The little American's blue eyes twinkled. "Never woke *him* up. I won't bother him tonight. I won't tell him about it till we get aboard that boat tomorrow." He fingered the crumpled letter in his pocket, and laughed softly. "And when I tell him about *this* he'll be pop-eyed—"

WILHELM SCHNEIDER, the beery Dutch planter from Islamahad, was pop-eyed. "Danger!" he gasped, sponging sweat from his three chins with a nervous handkerchief. "By the bones of the Queen, I should say there is danger! Too *verdammt* much of it to suit me. Whew! You did not tell the police. You sat and laughed. That letter! And then you are crazy to haff come on this boat, my friend. That letter. *Ach!* I am sick." He took a long, wheezy breath.

Leaning on the rail, Peter Scarlet gave a lazy smile. Small, comfortable in rumpled white drill, his larkspur-blue eyes twinkling with amused interest at the Malays crowding the deck below, he showed none of his fat friend's alarm. Peter Scarlet petted his snowy white beard; grinned.

"The letter doesn't scare me," he said quietly. "Asia's as full of cranks as a New York insane asylum. This crazy hoodoo letter—"

"Crazy? Hoodoo!" Schneider began to pant. "Here you haff told nobody about this note, and now we are on this lousy steamer with no chance of getting to land for three days. Better I would like it if we sat in the police bureau surrounded by police. Shades of Orange! And this demon has already shot at you. And you haff asked nobody for protection—"

"It's nonsense," said Scarlet, lounging into the deck chair

beside his friend, "to let a fool thing like this spoil our trip to Java. This freak crook was just tryin' to throw a scare at me, that's all. Why should I run to the police? If there is such a criminal as this fake, the police couldn't do anything. What, when you came right down to it finally, have they done to catch him so far?"

The fat Dutchman fanned his face with his sun helmet and glanced with apprehension up and down the deserted bridge deck. *"Gott im Himmel!* is not that just the trouble? This fiend is so clever the police haff been unable to catch him. From Singapore to Bangkok, Bombay to Yokohama has this monster been spreading fear. Why, he has worked almost a murder a month for the last year. The police haff no clues—nothing. They find dead men and that letter. They chase assassins but the right assassin always vanishes like a ghost. And now this man is after you and you just laugh—"

The Dutchman groaned, and mopped his face. "This is terrible."

"Don't get into a lather," Scarlet advised. "You know how the newspapers and police love to spread alarm." He fished in his pocket for the crumpled paper. "See for yourself the sort of Oriental rot it is."

Peter offered him the note.

Schneider took the note with shaky fingers, and read in a croaking whisper:

> To the Yankee with the white beard who is said to have purchased the Sacred Moons of Golan.
>
> Sahib:
> Leave the Moons in the brass water jar of the Mindar monkey temple tonight at midnight when no-one shall see, and go away. Do not return. Any attempt to advise the police, or your failure to obey this command will result in your death. Remember how many others have died. There is no escape from The Emperor of Death Who Wears The Beard."

A SHUDDER of fear escaped the Dutchman's lips. "Name of Wilhelmina! The same kind of warning as the others haff been. The Emperor of Death Who Wears The Beard—"

Scarlet laughed out loud. "There's a title for you. Sounds straight out of a penny serial. You see, I bought the Sacred Moons of Golan in the Mindar bazaar last week. Best string of black opals I ever saw in my life, an' worth every tikal that old Siamese trader soaked me for 'em. Yesterday morning this love letter arrives at the hotel. You see what it says. I'm to leave the opals in that stinking temple the other end of town at midnight, and just stroll away. Otherwise I'm doomed." The curio-hunter scoffed. "Think I'm falling for an old gag like that? Some Asian sharper heard I'd got the jewels an' thought he'd scare me out of them." He snorted contemptuously.

"And you didn't leave them at midnight," Schneider muttered, "so at three in the morning a bullet goes through your cuff. *Og heddon!* Then you get on this boat and laugh about this little letter and bullet—"

"The bullet missed, didn't it?" The little American curio-hunter smiled, his eye on a naked Malay sailor in the swinging foremast. A wave crunched against the steamer's bow, and a pleasantly cool bath of spray showered up to the bridge-deck. "Nothing to get sick about now," Scarlet went on. "I only showed you the letter because it's funny. The Emperor of Death Who Wears The Beard. It would take an Oriental to cook up a name like that—"

"*Gott!*" Schneider moaned. "The police say the killer *does* wear a beard." A startled oath broke from the Dutchman's teeth, and with a sudden gesture he yanked a heavy, blue Haenel automatic from his belt and dropped it into his lap. His finger's bit into Scarlet's arm, and his face turned the color of a damp melon. "Shades of Von Tromp! Look that way quick! Here comes one with a beard right now!"

CHAPTER II

THE TIGER CLAW

WESTWARD WHERE SUMATRA lay the sun wag a blazing cartwheel sinking in a sky of pure flame. Gold-red streamers of sunset bannered above the indigo sweep of Karimata Strait. The raffish mail steamer with its two decks of sooty cabins, its chattering fore-deck of Malay immigrants, its scraggly stern and bows and smoke-spouting funnel, was the only smirch against a perfect Asian sundown. The passenger who rounded the deck on the after quarter stopped to admire the view.

"*Ja!*" Schneider whispered fiercely. "With a beard—"

The traveler in question did have a beard. A neat white beard. His small frame also carried a trim pith helmet and wore a linen suit. His hand carried a Malacca stick and a small patent leather handbag. He threw a fistful of orange peels over the rail, turned and walked into one of the cabins ranged in a row with doors opening on the deck. Peter Scarlet lay back in his deck chair and guffawed loudly.

"Sure the man wore a beard. Like mine. What of it? You don't think that man is this emperor letter-writer, do you?" The little American curio-hunter shook his head, eyes bright. "Put up the gun, Wilhelm. That fellow is a medical missionary or something bound for the Celebes. I used to know him in Singapore. Wouldn't hurt a flea. Good Lord, we can't go batty at every whiskered mug we see from now till we make port. Why, there's seven men with whiskers on this hooker. There's two right now. That Malay *serang* an' the Asian bird of Paradise behind him—"

Peter Scarlet smiled, but Schneider sat with his automatic ready under his coat, eyes bulging stiff-lashed at the two who came up from below. The first was an Archipelago sailor, half-naked, fat, a faint growth of hair under his brass chin; bound to pick up a hawser from the scuppers. This *serang* was nothing but an ordinary Oriental; but the passenger coming along behind was not so ordinary.

Even for the East the passenger was unusual. A crimson mantle too hot for comfort fell to the heels. Scuffly slippers shuffled along too large for the feet. Head bound in an enormous peach-colored turban with a silver-mounted tiger's claw set in its peak. This costume was arresting, and the face of its wearer proved more so. It was not the curling black beard that rippled down from mouth and chin like lustrous brushings of silk. But the eyes were silky, too. Huge brown eyes with wide brown pupils. Benevolent and gentle as the eyes of a young doe.

The eyes made Scarlet think of two pieces of milk chocolate, and gave him a peculiar creep. He shifted his own stare to the tiger claw in the turban; then to the book in the wearer's brown hand. Scarlet noted the book was a vellum *Koran;* fastened his glance on the ring that bejeweled the little finger of the hand. A thrill went up Scarlet's spine. The little American knew his jewels, and he knew that ring was old. A genuine cabachon emerald worth a couple of fortunes.

The emerald flashed like a little green planet as its gorgeous wearer scuffled by, and Scarlet forgot where he was in the study of the fabulous-looking ring. The Asian's great moist eyes glanced sadly Scarlet's way, and the curio-hunter felt another shudder of distaste sneak into his veins. Scarlet held his own glance to the ring on that right hand, and it was Schneider who gave a grunt of dismay as the crimson-robed Oriental passed out of view around the deckhouse.

"You see him, Peter my friend? That cursed heathen? He looked all the time at you—"

"That Persian lamb?" Scarlet laughed. "Rigged up like a one-ring circus. These Asian boys certainly like to put on the dog. That bird's a Moslem priest of high order. Tiger claw ranks him next to Allah or something. Yeh. His eyes were like those of a damp fish. But that ring was worth looking at, an' I'd give my left lung to get one like it. That man is rich and how he loves to show it off. You'd never forget that costume."

The little curio-hunter admired the shadows where the Oriental had gone. "A good show—"

Schneider's fat hand caught tight on Scarlet's wrist. His face looked doughy. "Scarlet! If anybody could be like this Emperor of Death Who Wears The Beard it is that one who just passed. *Ja!* And you know something?" The Dutchman hoisted himself to his feet. "That man has the cabin right next to mine. So. And—*Herr Gott!* Who is it has the cabin next to you, did you tell me?"

PETER SCARLET stood up with a sigh. "Look here. We can't go on poking a nose at every passenger on this boat, thinking he's a demon killer. Forget this letter truckle. What if this Christmas-tree Moslem priest does have the cabin next yours? You can't accuse him because he has a beard. What Moslem hasn't? As for the cabin next to mine, the skipper told me it was taken by a Malay woman who came aboard two hours before we sailed, got seasick before we lifted the hook, and hasn't left her bunk since. A Malay princess or something. You see? You've let this bloody emperor hooey prey on your mind, Schneider. Forget it. The threat is nothing. You don't think any assassin would trail me on this boat to get those opals, anyhow. I put those opals in the Colonial Bank an hour after I bought 'em, and—"

"But this unknown killer with his beard has always trailed and slain the victims who did not obey him," the Dutchman panted. "He kills them as a warning to the next man he wishes to rob so. *Gott* knows how many haff been murdered. And the police cannot find the killer—"

"He's not on this craft," Scarlet said loudly, grinning. "Forget him. I want to enjoy the trip."

He went to the rail and watched a slim crescent moon brocade a silvery path through green clouds far in their wake. Darkness had come with tropic suddenness, and the sea was a black expanse of washing ebony water lit by silver streaks from the moon. On the fore-deck the Malays with their bundles and roosters and children were trying to soften the deck with blankets for the night. Up in the wheelhouse a sailor was whistling Chinese discords; and the boat shoved her heaving bows into a sceneless black that was almost cool.

"We'll sleep decently tonight," Scarlet went on. "Turn in early. Look now, Schneider, go do that unpacking of yours and quit worrying about whiskers and mash notes. I'm goin' to take a turn aft, an' I'll meet you in the smoking saloon at eight-thirty, see?"

He thumped a friendly knuckle on his fat companion's chest. "I appreciate your alarm about me, old man, but stow it. Emperor of Death? Bah. Don't forget. I'll be waiting in the smoke room at eight-thirty."

THE SMOKE room at eighty-thirty!

Peter Scarlet watched Schneider go into his cabin, bid him a genial good-evening, then turned on heel and moved like a cat down the deserted deck. Ten feet aft of Schneider's shuttered door the deck was black as a hat save for a faint pond of moonlight beyond the afterhouse. Hand on hip, the little American sped swiftly up the rail. He was not sure, but it seemed to him that cushioned feet had whispered down the ladder to the main-deck below; and he thought he saw a shadow melt into shadows farther aft.

The smoke room at eight-thirty.

"I hope I talked loud enough," Scarlet muttered to himself.

"It's eight-fifteen now. If my guess is right there'll be something doing in the smoke room a few minutes from now."

His guess was right. Something did happen. Only it happened in a terrible way.

He had not gained the bottom of the main-deck ladder when a soul-freezing scream spiralled up from the darkness amidships and ripped the hot gloom into a shower of echoing icicles.

CHAPTER III

FIRST BLOOD

"THE SMOKE ROOM. Already—"

A startled cry spewed from Scarlet's beard, echoing to join the dreadful caterwauling wails that made ghastly the dark. The hair reared stiff on the little curio-hunter's chin. Yanking his Lüger, he was down the lurching deck at a bound, cold eyes on the smoke room door from which the awful wailing seemed to come. On the deck overhead feet had started a running clatter, and voices called hoarse on the unseen bridge. Like a catamount Scarlet hurled himself through the saloon door; crashed into a pair of struggling figures.

A sea had started to run and the smoke room reeled. In the uncertainty shed by a dim ceiling lamp the battling pair crashed from tables to chairs in a wild waltz, and Scarlet danced in, trying to aim a shot. He was too late to do anything for the missionary with the white beard, though. Scarlet saw the knife in the man's bubbling throat, and even as the curio-hunter flung himself forward the missionary stopped shrieking and collapsed.

With a sharp cry, the missionary's assailant whipped a crimson mantle to cover his face and made a streak for the starboard entryway. Tripping on the dead padre's legs, Scarlet flopped to his face. His Lüger crashed, and with an explosion of shattered glass the ceiling lamp expired. But Scarlet's out-flung fist caught an ankle, and the robed assailant toppled crashing like a tackled dummy. Pounding fists in the pitch dark beat at Scarlet's face. Moans, the sound of ripping cloth and splintering wood. Scarlet drove out a fierce blow and shrieked as his knuckles struck wood. Teeth caught his hand, and a sharp set of fingernails lashed down his cheek as Scarlet fought to hold on and recover the Lüger lost in the scramble. It was no fun fighting over that corpse with the knife in its throat.

Scarlet couldn't find the gun. Fingernails were shredding his cheek and clawing at his eyes. A heel struck his jaw and stunned him, but his own battling fingers fastened in a flowing beard and held on. His bearded enemy screamed, kicked, bit and tore. Face smothered in hair, Scarlet struck out and missed again. His enemy screamed shrill falsetto, kicked out in the dark and drove a pointed toe into Scarlet's shin. The curio-hunter caught a hand and tried to twist a wrist. The hand got free, and with a terrific wrench that brought a frightful shriek the beard got free, too.

Lights were coming, now. Lights and pounding boots and clamoring voices. With a lunge, Scarlet, tried to fasten a new hold on his unseen opponent, missed, stumbled, struck his mouth, fell over a table. Before he could gain his feet the enemy had gone—a bat-like shadow hurtling across the floor to vanish in a gust of wind through the starboard door of the smoke room. The ship gave a lurch, and a wild cluster of frightened faces, waving hands and lanterns poured through the port door.

IT WAS Schneider, the Dutch planter, who dashed forward to hoist Scarlet to his feet; and when the lights had steadied the whole crowd stood aghast. The little missionary with the trim beard like Scarlet's was stone dead. Stabbed through the throat. The ship rolled and the dead missionary rolled; and Peter Scarlet glared at the fistful of glossy black hair in his left hand. Then he stared at the green, twinkly object in his right hand. The black beard! He had snatched some hair from that infernal black beard! And the emerald ring—

"The priest!" The shock of thought that burst in the back

of Scarlet's head made the cry that blew from his beard. "The Moslem priest with the black beard! He killed this man an' went out that door. Quick! Schneider! Th' rest of you! Come on. I'm going to get that Moslem killer if it's th' last thing I ever do—"

Peter Scarlet ran as he had never run before, with the Dutchman close behind and the rest of the pack yapping along in the blinding dark. A nice obstacle race past stanchions, water buckets, coiled hawser and deck bits waiting to trip the unwary. A race for the after ladder that led topside.

Salty wind whipped perspiration from the little American's forehead. His hand was an iron knot on his gun. And he clutched the emerald ring in a fist like a vise. Schneider saw the fury shining like phosphor in Scarlet's eye.

"The Emperor of Death with the Beard!" The name panted from the Dutchman's white lips, and his face was a wet round moon in the gloom.

"The priest!" Scarlet squalled over his shoulder. "The one with the black beard an' brown eyes. That devil! He stabbed the padre. I'll get him if I die at it! The fiend thought the missionary was *me*. Get it? Overheard me say I was goin' to the smoke room. Beat it down there an' met the missionary comin' in. What a break for the poor padre. That devil thought it was me. Mistook the priest for me—in the dark— We'll get that cur—"

"He tried to kill you!"

"And stabbed the missionary." Scarlet groaned as he ran. "All my fault. My scheme. Thought I'd talk loud an' then see if anybody tried to sneak down to the smoke room to spot me. Just goin' down to see if anybody was around when I heard the scream. Quick—"

OVER ON the port beam of the ship a crowd of sailors were shouting, and the uproar spread to the bows. "Murder! Murder!" Somewhere aloft a man squalled orders and a mate's whistle shrilled. Feet flayed the bridge-deck; and just as the little curio-hunter and the Dutchman jumped for the after ladder a bulky figure with a lantern came thumping down the steps. The light picked out a beet-red face, Scotch as a pint of whisky. A square face with a jutting, bumpy red nose, sideburns stiff as military brushes, and stony eyes under the visor of a white sea cap. Angus Burl, the captain.

The hard eyes fastened on the gun in Scarlet's fist. "What the devil's going on here?"

The little curio-hunter's eyes were hard, too. "Murder. In the smoking saloon. Passenger. The missionary. Stabbed in the throat. That Moslem priest with the black beard killed him. Saw him do it."

"He's the Emperor of Death!" Schneider was jigging and screaming. *"Lieber Gott—"*

"Good Lord!" The skipper's face was astonished. "You mean the gaudy heathen in the red robe—"

"Quick!" Scarlet shouted. "He ran this way. May have tried to get on the upper deck—"

"Sure he did!" The captain yelled a curse. "He strolled past me just as I was coming down. Didn't look in a hurry. Walked for his cabin—"

Peter Scarlet made a grab for the ladder. A cool devil, this assassin. Makes a dash for his life by strolling past the skipper and calmly walking for his cabin. Sweat poured down the curio-hunter's cheeks, and his hand on the automatic was icy cold. Schneider was sweating, too. His beefy back was wet across the shoulders. He climbed fast behind Scarlet, and the Scotch skipper and the rest of the crowd came along in the rear yelling like fools.

The bridge-deck was deserted, shadowy in the night. A sooty pall of smoke lingered over the monkey bridge above the wheel house. A faint green glow sifted along the rail, coming from the starboard light. A streak of yellow came from the chart room and lit up the row of closed cabin doors, six silent doors facing the deck. Moonbeams confused the remaining shadows, touching brasswork with a faint shine.

The crowd behind Scarlet went deadly silent as the curio-hunter pointed at the stateroom last in line—the cabin next to Schneider's. On the decks below there was a hullabaloo, and the only other sound was the surge of floundering water and dim thud of engines.

"That cabin—"

"Look careful!"The captain panted, gesturing a pistol. A figure in shirtsleeves appeared on the wing of the monkey bridge. "Hi!" the skipper called at the mate on watch. "You, mister. You see that heathen priest go into that cabin there just as I ran below?"

The man on the bridge-wing shook his head. "Nobody, sir. I thought th' riot was below, an' I had me eye on the decks for'ard."

"Well, that's where he was headin' when he went by me," the skipper snarled. "Break in that door!"

CHAPTER IV

THE VANISHER

THE CROWD EDGED back, a panting circle. Gun steady, eyes like nail heads polished to shine, Peter Scarlet hurled a shoulder at the white door.

"Keep back!"

Schneider drove a boot at the shuddering panel, and the wood splintered.

"Careful now!"

Again the curio-hunter drove a blow at the wooden barrier and the door fell inward with a splintering crash. Scarlet's automatic slammed twice, speeding bullets into the dark interior. But there came no answering fire, no answering scream. When the echoes and smoke had cleared and the skipper's lantern cast a ray through the broken casement there was nothing inside to be seen. Nothing. Just a barren cabin with unruffled bunk, fresh-painted walls, an empty shelf, a washstand punctured by two fresh bullet holes where Scarlet's shots had gone.

Scarlet whirled around. "The other cabins. Quick. He couldn't have gone far. He must be up here. We were right behind him. If he ran over to the port side and beat it down the forward ladder the man on the bridge would have seen him."

The captain bellowed. "That's right. He's right here on this bridge-deck. Only place he could have come without being spotted. He must be in one of these six staterooms. Break 'em in!"

"That's my cabin!" Schneider yelled, flinging open the next door. The cabin was lighted, and the creamy glow streamed out to catch the glint of guns and sweating faces. The Dutchman rushed in and out with an agile bound. "Not there. *Herr Gott—*"

Scarlet's cabin, number three, was also empty. Meantime the captain had beat his way into number five, the cabin the slain missionary had occupied, to find it also deserted. A sailor slammed through into six, the last cabin aft, and reported it vacant. A taut-nerved suspense strung the gloom. The crowd along the rail made a row of twisting faces, weird as Chinese masks in the shifting light. The Scotch skipper's face was twisting with dark rage. Schneider's round countenance was pop-eyed. Little rivers of sweat rippled down Peter Scarlet's cheeks as he lifted his automatic, steadied the glinting barrel, growled hoarsely.

"There's only one more cabin. Number four. Th' one next to mine here. That's th' last cabin. Th' only one left where this devil could've gone—"

"But there's a woman in there," the skipper snarled. "I saw her go in before we left port. Native princess by the looks. She shut herself in when we sailed an' hasn't been seen since." Stepping up to the door, the Scotchman beat a tattoo with his knuckles. "Hey, you in there!" Abruptly his voice changed to a roar. "Open that door an' open it quick! We know he's in there with you. Open that door—"

FOR A moment the only answer was a stifled silence. And then the reply came through the barrier startling as a bolt from the blue. A soft feminine voice, gentle and constrained, speaking clear English. "One moment please."

Peter Scarlet's mouth fell open. Schneider gasped. A baffled expression crossed the skipper's face. "Why, she was veiled an' wearin' th' clothes of a native woman!" And even before those words had left the captain's startled mouth the door of Number Four cabin swung open, and the lady stood on the threshold. The little American curio-hunter felt something happen to his insides. The gun lowered in his shaky hand. A lady, yes. And what a lady!

If Peter Scarlet knew his curios, he also knew his ladies. He had seen some beautiful Orientals in his day, from the sacred dancers of Bangkok to the milk-skinned beauties of the Circassian hills. But never had he seen one to equal in face or form the woman who stood in that tilting cabin doorway and let her eyes smile softly into his. The little curio-hunter drew a breath, and so did the men behind him.

Once in a thousand years an artist caught such a figure in ivory. The graceful arms were like something soft in native brass. Her hair was spun bronze. A thin veil made a shade over mouth, chin and throat, but could not hide the curve of the perfect chin and the bow of the ruby warm lips. Oriental as Asia, and feminine as Mother Eve with tiny satin slippers on feet made to dance for the gods and pendant brass earrings in ears like petals of rose. And when the woman looked at Peter Scarlet he knew he had never seen such eyes. Soft eyes deep as the blue Jihan wells.

"You wish to look in my cabin?" She smiled at Scarlet, and her voice was sweeter than the music of a Japanese water bell. "Somebody you seek? But nobody is in my cabin. Please see for yourself. I am sorry. Is something wrong?"

Peter Scarlet looked into her cabin. There was a small shelf on which a small native handbag sat. A bamboo parasol stood folded against the shallow bunk. A transparent silk shawl hung on one wall above a tiny pair of silver slippers. A powder box and jeweled lady's comb were on the washstand. Scarlet glared at the golden-skinned woman with the well-deep eyes, ruby mouth and tumbled bronze hair; glared into her cabin again. The Moslem priest was not to be seen, and there was no place where he could have hidden. Then he wasn't in there. Not a sign of him. He should have been in that cabin, and he was not.

The little American curio-hunter brushed a damp hand across his forehead. He had seen some Asian mysteries in his day; but even in Asia a Moslem priest with a silky black beard and bulging brown eyes and slim hands wet with his victim's blood couldn't vanish in thin air. A shiver trickled down Peter Scarlet's spine. Something was wrong, all right.

"JA, SO. *Ja,* so." Schneider was wringing his hands. "It is like I haff told you, Peter. This Emperor of Death is like one ghost. Haff not the police of a dozen lands given chase and lost him like a puff of smoke? *Gott im Himmel!* He has killed the missionary by mistake. Who will be next?"

"Nobody!" Scarlet shouted. "Get a move on those sailors of your's, Cap'n Burl. Fast. Run 'em over every nook an' cranny of th' ship. That killer's aboard, an' we'll get him. Search th' holds, main-deck, bows, bridge." The little American's voice banged like a gun. His white beard was out stiff as tin, eyes snappering in the lamp-light. "Sweep the ship!"

The Scotchman shouted and his mate came bounding down from the monkey bridge. "Wake up, Mister! Shotguns! Lanterns! Turn out all hands! Whole damned crew to get busy. Engine room stand by. There's a murderer on this ship. May be that desperate killer we heard about back in Singapore." The skipper turned on Scarlet. "You think it's this Emperor of Death?"

Scarlet wiped his face. "Yes. After me, though. The missionary looked like me an' got stabbed by accident. We've got to be careful. This fiend stops at nothing. Tried to kill me in Mindar. Nobody on this boat will be safe till we've cornered that priest. Tell your men to shoot on sight!"

The Emperor of Death! The name went from mouth to

mouth and became a weird sort of cry. As if a cold wind was breathing on the men who jostled on the swinging upper deck. Among the wavering shadows the captain's face was a cursing cartoon, Schneider was a sweating moon with butterfly hands, Scarlet's eyes were steel points. And there, in the bright-lighted doorway of Number Four cabin, stood that Asian beauty, wide-eyed, golden, tremulous, like some misty Peri transferred into a scene of horror from a scented rose garden in Nirvana. And as "The Emperor of Death! The Emperor of Death killed that missionary!" went from mouth to mouth in wild refrain, the golden woman seemed to sway. Suddenly her hands went to her gauze-veiled lips and she cried out:

"The missionary? The nice little missionary? He is the one who has been killed?" A sob broke from her lips, and she caught at Scarlet's sleeve. "Terrible!" her voice was low. "I am sorry. He was my friend. Let me help you." Her eyes flashed lambent fire. "Let me help you find the demon who could slay my friend—"

Peter Scarlet spun on the skipper. "Everybody must help! Get your men into the hold. Look into every cabin. Quick! Schneider, stay with me. We'll go over this deck again. Go through these cabins. Comb every corner—"

"The boat's yours!" Captain Burl grabbed Scarlet's hand. "You know more about this assassin than I do. I'll run my crew below. Got to look after th'dead man, too. We'll round up that murderer if he's aboard."

The skipper's voice squalled orders. Dusky seamen padded along the rail, shotguns glinting in their hands. Mates and wheelmen were already hunting through the quarters on the bridge, poking their guns into chart rooms and cabins. On the fore-deck the Malay immigrants were wailing with alarm as the *serang* and his men kicked through their ranks.

PETER SCARLET watched the captain and his men swarm down the after ladder. A shadow slipped past Scarlet's elbow, and the silk-veiled woman was after the others, her bronze hair blowing and her feet twinkling in and out of light pools. Just as she reached the ladder, she turned her eyes on Scarlet and cried out. "I must help, too. The missionary was my friend—"

The deck rolled and a gust of spray wet the woman's face so that it shone, and then she had gone from sight. Scarlet flung on Schneider with a curse. "Quick! Into her cabin. He must have gone in there. There may have been another way out. A door under her bunk—"

But there was no other way out. No door under the bunk. Nothing. Followed by the panting Dutchman, Scarlet flung down the line of cabins again. Number Six. Number Five. The woman's again. Then into his own and into Schneider's and into the one the priest had occupied. No exit save the doors that had been kicked in. No trace of the missing priest with the long black beard. Baffled growls leaked from Scarlet's beard, and the Dutchman sagged with a fright he did not try to conceal.

A sailor came up from below to report that the killer had not been located on the main-deck or forward holds. The mate called down from the monkey bridge. "Nothing doing."

"They won't find him hiding in the after hold, either," Scarlet cried, stopping to lean for breath on the rail. The sea was mounting and salt spray flew in the dark. The little American watched an indigo wave swing abeam and collapse in a froth of white lace. The ship trembled, plodding through the blackness under an umbrella of ghostly smoke. A few faint stars high overhead and the thin crescent moon fading out far behind. Somehow that mystic moon matched the spell that seemed to have enwrapped the boat. The curio-hunter fingered his gun. "There's something funny here, Schneider. Something so cursed awful that when we find it out it'll be worse than any black magic you ever heard of."

WILHELM SCHNEIDER, the beery Dutch planter from Islamahad, groaned heavily. "The Emperor of Death with the Beard. *Ach Gott!* I haff been afraid for—"

An oath blew from Scarlet's clenched teeth. "I had him, too. That wasn't any fake beard, either. I pulled th' hair out by the roots. And those big eyes. It was that priest, all right. But a man *can't* vanish." The curio-hunter's voice panted. Black wind swept up from the water and wet his face. The ship trembled and chugged to a sound of straining timber and creaking blocks. Far below in the after hold boots were running and voices shouted faintly. Scarlet glared at the Asian dark and whispered. "Queer. Something queer happened up on this deck, Schneider. This priest with his beard—"

A sharp cry shrilled from the Dutchman's throat. *"Gott!"*

Scarlet spun round, and saw Schneider stagger against the rail. Steel glinted in the Dutchman's shoulder. The curio-hunter gasped. A knife, long, lean, needle-thin stiletto was buried to the hilt in Schneider's shoulder. Blood welled like red enamel around the quivering hilt. The Dutchman's face was gray in the gloom, and he fought to keep his feet. Two inches farther toward his neck and that flung blade would have killed him.

"Thrown!" Scarlet yelled. "From where!"

In the darkness who could tell? But it must have come from aft. Somewhere in the direction of the after ladder feet were running with a cat-soft, echo-y sound. Hand sweating on his gun, Scarlet charged the after ladder and went chin-banging to the dark deck below.

CHAPTER V

KNIVES IN THE NIGHT

IT WAS NO place to chase a murderer, that afterdeck swathed in darkness and tipping steeper at each fresh assault from the East India seas. A shower of black water took Scarlet in the face as he vaulted down the tilting ladder, and his first bound took him crashing into an unseen winch. The little American curio-hunter bounced to his feet, and strove to pierce the swinging darkness. A deck house and an awning hung over the stern, and the after hatchway made a dim yellow square in the black.

Zing! Something shiny sped out of the shadows beyond the hatch. A chill breeze whistled past Scarlet's ear. The shiny streak of death struck the ship's rail with a burst of little sparks and carommed on out to sea. *Bzzang!* Another one. Just in time Scarlet dropped to his knees, and the hurtling knife spun over his head to vanish in the black beyond the rail. The assassin was hiding near that deck house and hurling stilettos. Scarlet fell flat on his stomach. The third knife scissored a shred from his collar, struck in the scuppers and flew out across the water. That one was cursed close. Peter Scarlet flung himself behind the winch, swung his gun, let fly.

Crash! Crash! Crash! The gunfire tore the black with spurts of bright flame as the curio-hunter sent six shots ripping from port to starboard, a scythe of bullets that swept a deadline across the afterdeck. A wild chorus of yells came up out of the lighted hatch, and a frantic clamor rose on the ladder leading up from the hold. But the dark figure that raced from the bullet-lashed gloom to run like the wind around the deck house and vanish in the direction of the taffrail made no sound at all.

Scarlet's feet flew aft in wild chase. Loading his Lüger as he ran, the little American tore after the dim figure he had seen, heedless of the knife that might greet him as he rounded the ship's rolling stern. There was no one waiting for him at the taffrail. His enemy had kept on going around the deck house. Now a thousand feet seemed to be pounding out of the deck house hatch, and voices and lights were coming from all directions. Charging around the corner of the deck house, the curio-hunter tripped on a wheel-chuck, floundered, fell flat. A voice cried out, and slim hands reached for his arm. Unsteady on his feet, Scarlet found himself facing the woman with the bronze hair and Circe eyes.

HER VOICE was eloquent with alarm. "You were running? What is wrong? Are you hurt?"

The deck slipped under Scarlet's feet, and her silken body

was soft against him. He pushed away her arm. "You! Where'd you come from?"

"Up from below. I was behind the others and heard shooting. So I ran up here. Oh, this is terrible, terrible. I am frightened—" In the darkness her face was a pale oval lit by deep, scared eyes; and Scarlet could see her smooth chin trembling beneath the gauzy Oriental veil. "Did you see him? Did you see this dreadful murderer!"

Scarlet caught her arm with a hand like a vise. "Did *you* see him? Speak! He came around this way. I was right behind him. If you were just coming out of that hatchway you must have seen him—"

"But I saw nobody! I saw you come around the deck, but nobody was in front of you. I thought they must be chasing you!"

The scared voice was drowned by a chorus of shouting; and before Scarlet could release her arm the crowd was dancing around him. "What's wrong?"—"You get 'im?"—"We just come outa th' hold. There wasn't nobody hiding there!" Lanterns shed streaks of yellow through the wild darkness, and Peter Scarlet fought to control brains that wanted to spin like a bird's nest in a hurricane. This wasn't real. This was madness. The murderer had tossed knives at him from the shadows forward of the deck house. He had chased the killer around the ship's stern. Once more the assassin had vanished like a whisk of smoke.

Captain Burl plunged out of the crowd and caught at Scarlet's shoulder. "What the devil! That shooting! We were all down in the hold. Went over every inch below an' didn't find this killer. Where is he?"

"Up on this main-deck," Scarlet howled. "Threw a knife from the top of the after ladder and struck Schneider in the shoulder. I chased after, but couldn't see him. Knives came at me like bullets. I fired into the shadows but missed. Saw a figure—couldn't tell who—come around the deck house, here, and chased. Ran clean around the house an' bumped into this woman comin' my way.

Somewhere in between that Moslem murderer disappeared. Just plain vanished. But he put a knife into my friend—"

THE HULLABALOO that went up then was something to drown the sound of hammering waves. Sailors glared at each other and clutched tighter their shotguns. The Scotch skipper wiped a streak of water from his red chin. A sort of sob came from the golden-skinned woman with the lambent eyes; and Schneider the Dutchman came shoving through the waving fringe of arms, his eyes moony with alarm. His left arm hung limp under a bandaged shoulder, and his Haenel automatic swung nervously in his right fist.

"Du Lieber Gott im Himmel! Scarlet, did you get him? I heard you shooting. Haff you found the murderer? A damn on him, for my shoulder screams with pain. But just a flesh wound. The knife came out easy. What! You haff not cornered yet this devil?"

"Get going!" Scarlet ground out through his teeth. "Quick, before he gets planted an' drives a blade into somebody. He's around this deck, by God. Maybe anywhere. If we don't draw a bead on him soon—"

"There's something damned queer going on aboard here!" The roar came from the Scotch captain, and he swung his lantern at Scarlet's face. "One of my passengers is murdered in cold blood, an' you can't tell where the thug went. Then this Moslem priest who strolls by me manages to disappear. We hunt him down below, an' you stay behind an' claim somebody scaled knives at you an' this Dutchman. But you chase the knife-thrower an' he's vanished, too, somewhere between you and this woman right here on this afterdeck. You claim it's this criminal th' papers ashore been howling about. This Emperor of Death—"

"Look!" The scream that interrupted the captain's bellowing came from the woman. She was standing at the rail and pointing a slim finger at something she had seen over the side. In the darkness and leaping shadow-and-light she was like an ivory carving, and her voice came clear as a bell above the furore of pounding water and noisy men. "Look down there!"

It was barely visible, wrapped about a length of rope that dangled from the wheel-chuck set in the deck above. A stray shine from a lantern touched the cloth, and the wet strip of cambric flagged like a piece of gay laundry above the tumbling water. But it was no mere piece of laundry that hung there wound around that dangling length of rope. It was a strip of peach-colored cloth that hung there, and the light from the wavering lanterns fell on a shiny little silver-mounted tiger's claw caught in the dripping folds.

CHAPTER VI

THE FINGER OF FATE

SCARLET, SCHNEIDER, CAPTAIN Burl and the woman leaned far over the tipping ship's rail to glare at the bannering wet rag. With a sharp oath the Scotch skipper snatched at the rope and fished the drenched cloth to the deck; held it, dripping, close to a lantern. The little American curio-hunter yelled, then.

"Th' Moslem priest's turban. That's what it is. He took it off and threw it over the rail an' the wind caught it onto that rope hanging overside. That's it. That's the turban he was wearing. By heaven, don't you see? This fiend shed his costume and chucked it overboard!"

"Or perhaps he went overboard himself," Schneider yelled hopefully. "*Gott!* Maybe so that is how he vanishes between you running one way and this woman coming the other, *hein?* So. He jumps over the side and this turban catches on. Where else could he haff gone?"

"But if he jumped over this rail aft here," Scarlet barked, "and his turban came off, the wind would have carried it beyond the stern and it'd have sunk. No. That turban was flung overside the top deck—the bridge deck on this side of the ship. That's where he tossed it over—"

"Or that's where *he* went over," the skipper snarled.

"But he didn't go over amidships," Scarlet yelled. "I was chasing him around this deck house not forty seconds after he tossed those blades at me. I—"

"And you claim," the Scotch skipper snarled hoarsely, "that this knife-thrower vanished between you and the woman coming out of the hatch as she says. No. That Moslem priest hasn't been on this boat since we hunted through those cabins up there. I say he went overside. Amidships like you say. Yes. I bloody well know he went overside, or we'd have sighted him somewhere on this ship." The Scotchman's voice rose shrill as a saw, and the eyes went hard as flint in his beet-hued face. "That's it. The Moslem priest went overside, I say. An' what's more, I say somebody *chucked* him overside!"

"The devil you do!" Scarlet gasped. "Then who threw those knives at me down on this after deck? Who plugged that knife into this man Schneider? Who did I chase around this deck house not four minutes—"

Angus Burl was a big man. He put his chest close to Scarlet's, and backed the little American curio-hunter against the swaying deck house wall. "How should I know?" and his voice was like a file on iron. To Scarlet's amazement the Scot's pistol was planted against his stomach. The fily voice rasped on.

"How should I know, eh? But one thing Angus Burl knows. A Moslem priest nor nobody vanishes like a ghost on a ship at sea nor anywhere. Now get this! You claim to have run into that smoke room an' found this killer strugglin' with th' missionary, drivin' a knife into his throat. Th' lights go out, says you. You fight with th' Moslem an' he gets clear of you an' runs away. Th' crowd comes in an' you give chase. I see this Moslem head for his cabin. We run back up there but he ain't there. You kick open th' stateroom door, fire two shots, look in, say they ain't no bloody person inside. We look in all the other cabins an' find nobody but this woman. You sat topside while we runs below an' don't find a trace of this heathen holy man. Then what? While I'm below with me men I hear shootin'. I run topside an' find you chasin' around th' deck after a man who ain't to be found. That's *your* story, mister!"

"My story!" Scarlet snapped fiercely. "What the seven devils do you mean?"

"I mean," shouted the Scotchman, his voice mounting to a roar, "I mean it's too damned thin. Too phoney. Too bloody queer. I mean I don't believe it. I mean this here Moslem priest didn't have nothin' to do with stabbin' that missionary maybe. Sure, man! How do I know you didn't go inside that smoke room an' stab him yourself!"

"Myself!" Scarlet cried and threw up a hand.

"YOURSELF!" THE skipper bawled. "Yes. You might've stabbed that missionary. Who else was there around? Didn't my men run in there an' find you alone with the body in the dark? Then you says it's this Moslem who strolls by me on the upper deck. We rush after the Moslem. You break into the cabin, fire two shots, look in, say it's empty. We beat into the other cabins. Yeh. The priest ain't to be seen. Why? Because you shot him dead an' he's lyin' yet in a corner of his cabin where we don't spy him. Then what? You send us all runnin' below. You stay behind with this Dutchman, eh? What do you do? You throw the body overside, that's what! The ship's in an uproar an' nobody sees the splash.

"Then what do you do, mister? Why, you put a knife in your Dutch fellow to establish a nice fake alibi. You make a fake run across the afterdeck pretending to shoot at a figure you seen. You say this figure threw knives at you? Where are those knives, eh? Sure. You'll say they all flew overboard. But it's too bloody thin. That priest never vanished up on that bridge deck. It won't go. I say you jettisoned him overside. I say you tried to pin the missionary's murder on that Moslem. You tried to pull this vanishing yarn twice, an' it don't work. I say—"

"Wait!" It was the woman who cried out; stepped forward with slim hands trembling against her cheeks. Her strange, pool-deep eyes were on Scarlet. A sob broke from her trembling, thin-veiled lips. She pointed a slim, dark hand straight at the American's stunned face. A hand that trembled like a dove's wing in the bright lantern-shine.

"Wait," she whispered in a voice that tried to be loud. "I know. I remember now. The good white captain may be right. Listen. This man and his Dutch friend did stay behind on the bridge. I was last one down the ladder, following the rest of you. When I looked back I saw them start toward the cabins, again. Then I hurried down the ladder and crossed the deck, not wishing to be left behind in the dark." Her voice came clear, accusing. "It was then—it was then I thought I saw a black shape come down from the deck above. It struck the water. There seemed to be a splash. I could not be sure. I—"

"Ach Gott!" Schneider shrieked, jumping and wheezing. "False it is to accuse Herr Scarlet and me. Nonsense. We did not stay behind and throw over any dead body. There was nobody in that cabin the priest owned. *Nein!* And you think I drive a knife into my own shoulder for the joke? *Ja, ja!* Mad you all are! Mad! The Emperor of Death is on this boat. He wrote my friend a letter. The Emperor of Death—"

Peter Scarlet's wild yell was unexpected, right then. Backed against the deck house wall with the sweat pouring down his face, the skipper's gun in his ribs and mad voices beating in his ears, an expression akin to madness had come to the little curio-hunter's face. Did he see the knotted face of the Scotch captain with its blazing eyes? Did he hear Schneider's frantic protest? He did not! The little curio-hunter stood there glaring at the slim hand of the woman who had accused him, and the yell that broke from his teeth came like a cannon-shot!

"Stop! One minute, you fools! Captain Burl, let me go! Give me three minutes to prove, and by heaven I'll hand this Emperor of Death over to you to be hanged!"

But a fierce growl exploded from the Scotch-skipper's teeth. "The devil you will! And you won't get three minutes! You've played enough hell around already. The Emperor of Death, eh? Didn't the police call him The Emperor of Death Who Wears the Beard? So. That was this criminal's name. And the papers claimed he wore the beard, too. All right. *You* got a beard, ain't you? And you killed this missionary, eh? And the Moslem to cover your tracks, too. Three minutes to kill somebody else in, eh? Well, you don't get three minutes for nothing at all. If anybody's an Emperor of Death on this craft of mine it's *you! An' into the irons you go!*"

Speaking of irons! A blue barrel of metal whipped upward with the force of cold dynamite and crashed like a bludgeon on Captain Angus Burl's Scotch chin.

CHAPTER VII

THE DOOM ABOVE

FAT MEN ARE known to be agile, but no fat man ever drove a quicker blow than the smash Wilhelm Schneider landed with his gun barrel on that Scotchman's surprised chin. A mighty lucky move for the curio-hunter. Those sailors and Malays crowding behind their captain had given an ugly, tigerish growl when the skipper had painted Scarlet as The Emperor of Death. Some of them had lifted their guns. But Schneider's wallop flung the skipper over like a sack of grain, and the sailors went down like tangling tenpins. The golden woman gave a soprano scream. A pistol crashed and a hot bullet whipped through Peter Scarlet's sleeve. Lanterns smashed in bursts of smoke and oil, and the deck was a kaleidoscope of screaming mouths, floundering arms and mad noise.

It was touch and go for the curio-hunter and the Dutchman, then. Scarlet got over the pile-up at one bound, battling to kick hands from his ankles. The bawling Schneider booted a pair of shins. The woman stood against the rail with her hands against her face, lips screaming.

"Shoot th' Yankee! Th' Dutchman! Kill 'em both!" From the bottom of the wild tangle the skipper squalled. *Crack! Smash!* A pistol and a shotgun fired, and bullets ripped. The furious sailors came up off the deck shouting; the captain screeching like the vortex of a cyclone. Guns flamed and a rain of hot lead scattered around the Dutchman and Yankee. No time to linger. With a cry Scarlet fled around the corner of the deck house, Schneider after him, and the cyclone screaming and banging at Schneider's heels.

Next second the whole furore was blattering down the after hatch, bullets singing over Scarlet's ducking head and punching holes in the Dutchman's flagging coat-tails. A wave of heat smote the curio-hunter in the face as he turned down an alleyway. He caught his companion's arm.

"We've got to beat the race. They'll shoot us to sponge. Quick! Our only chance. The forward hold—"

It was no fun racing down that unfamiliar alleyway in the heart of that reeling mail ship with the crew and captain gunning along like fury close behind. The roar of the gunfire clanged like breaking iron doors in the confined space between bulkheads. Powder smoke billowed in the ventilators, and the hot air dinned with shouts and pounding feet. Down one corridor and up another the curio-hunter and the Dutchman dodged, ducking bullets that whistled over their heads, ricocheted like bees off iron plates, bounced and skidded off walls and flooring.

SCARLET SHOVED his gasping friend through a bulkhead that led amidships, and slammed the casement. But he could not throw the bar to lock the bulkhead shut, and just managed to race up the corridor before the iron door flew open and the shooting crew tumbled through. Now they had to make a dash for it. One long corridor with another closed bulkhead at its end. Near the bulkhead an open hatchway dropped to the engine room. A smell of steaming oil flowed from the hot, yellow aper-

ture, and a stoker with a wisp of rag around his throat stood
black and naked in the companionway and watched Scarlet
come toward him. The stoker's mouth fell open as the little
American and the Dutchman ran at him. At the aft end of the
alleyway a hooting swarm of sailors tumbled over each other
and fired guns. The ship rolled and the corridor gave a lurch.
Flashing and stunning noise shook the close walls, and bullets
skimmed through smoke.

No time to open that closed bulkhead leading to the forward
hold. Scarlet screamed at the Dutchman, and flung himself at
the stoker in the open hatch. The coal-blacked fireman went
spinning against a wall. Schneider squalled in Dutch. Scarlet
shouted. Then the two of them were pounding down a long iron
ladder into a well of terrific heat and grinding din; down the
ladder and along an iron grating, and down another ladder and
into a room of thudding machines and pounding pistons and
grinding steel arms.

At the top of the companionway the sailors knelt to shoot
down through the grating. Lead pellets bounced off steel shafts
and spun into galloping flywheels. Powder smoke floated
through heat waves and sprays of scattering engine-oil. The
skipper leaned over the ladder rail, steadied his pistol and fired
twice. One bullet knocked the heel from Scarlet's left boot,
almost throwing him off balance into a hammering set of brass-
shiny pistons. By this time the engine crew had decided to get
in the battle and were swarming down iron ladders and grill
ledges like greasy monkeys. With the crew on the companion
ladder and the engineers closing in from all sides, escape from
that hot den of machinery was cut off.

Scarlet pointed at a little iron door, and howled. "The stoke
hole. Our only way of escaping these confounded madmen—"

But before his hand touched the stokehole door the iron
plate swung inward. A blast of furnace heat and blazing red
light smote the curio-hunter and the Dutchman full in the eyes.
And a gigantic blackamoor with a wicked shotgun in his sweat-
dripping fists stepped out of the fire room and barred the door.

Above the thunderous drumming of the turbines, the clank of machinery, the spitting of hot steam and the clack of racing boots, the Scotch skipper's voice rang hoarse as an old bugle.

"Blacky! Shoot those two men—"

Something had to happen right then. And it did.

BLACKY SWUNG his shotgun to shoot those two men, and the two men cried out, and the giant stoker's weapon never fired. For a strange and uncanny sound broke like the echo of a distant storm in the engine room din. An outcry that came from the topside decks of the heaving mail ship. A wild chorusing scream, like the concert shrieking of a hundred frantic men. The screaming loudened in pitch, grew in volume, shrill and many-voiced. On the decks above the engine room a thousand feet seemed to be milling, making a sound like the scurrying of a million terrified rats. Somewhere up there a gun had started to pop. The screaming grew to a roar.

Next moment a white figure in shirtsleeves burst through the hatch at the top of the engine room companion. The skipper and his men had been halfway down the iron ladder, peppering with their guns; but they turned to stare at the shirtsleeved figure of the mate, and then continued to stare. The woman, who had been close behind the skipper on the ladder, gave a cry and almost fell. The engineers on the grating yelled.

That mate was something to holler about, too. A knife had gashed him from forehead to chin and his mouth was a crimson streak in his face.

"The Malays!" He tottered on the high ladder, waving sick hands, voice coming like steam from a smashed siren. "The Malay immigrants! They've heard this killer was on board an' gone wild."

The words choked out in the seaman's bloodied throat. In the corridor beyond him there exploded a vasty roar. The ship pitched and shook as the screw spun out of water and the engine raced, and before she righted herself a horde of brown men had boiled through the engine-hatchway. Twisty wet faces, frenzied brown hands waving sharp, curved knives, poured, shrieking, through the hatch. If the engine room had been filled with crazy sounds before it was a maniac dinning now.

Peter Scarlet laughed out loud and swung his automatic fast. *Slam! Slam! Slam!* He fired from the hip, but he did not shoot at the dumfounded Negro stoker who had forgotten to explode the shotgun. Scarlet's gun jumped hot in his hand, and the bullets whistled at a black box set into the starboard wall. The black box spouted a crackly blue flame. There was a puff of smoke and a stench of burnt fuses, and, as if doused by a monster hand, every light in that hollering engine room went out to plunge the uproar into darkness.

CHAPTER VIII

THE CABIN CLUE

IT WAS A real uproar, then. A raving Gehenna stunned by the clanking of marine machines and the shrieks of men, lit only by the evil flash of gunfire and the sullen square of maroon that marked the door of the fire room. Grabbing at Schneider's arm, Peter Scarlet got away from that betraying stoke-hole hatch; went stumbling through the blind dark for the companion. A strange little picture of Hades that engine room was, with the Malays rioting in the hatch aloft, sailors and engineers and a mad skipper and a golden woman rushing about in the dark below, the engines booming and guns snappering and here and there a flash of gunflame shedding lightning on a cranking steel piston or whirring wheel.

"The Malays!"—"The Emperor of Death!"—"Where are they!"—"Hey, Blacky! Blacky!"—"They're throwing them knives!"—"Keep back!"—"Where's the woman!"—"Shoot through that grating!"—"Keep clear o' that shaft!"—"Where's that Yankee an' Dutchman!" Frantic voices interwoven in a crazy medley. Somebody shrieking like a cat. Shadows swinging on the companion ladder. Men like black ghosts leaping from ladder-rungs to gratings. Wraiths rushing by in the furnace-hot dark.

Scarlet's hand was a trap on Schneider's wounded arm, and his words ground low through clenched teeth. "Stay with me. We'll get clear in th' riot. Mind your hand. Those pistons. That stoker's lost us. There's an alley under here. Come on."

The little curio-hunter's feet skidded on oily iron. Fumbling along a metal wall full of boltheads, he picked his way past a thudding piston rod, leading Schneider through a dark maze where oil splashed. Around them the world might have gone storming mad. Yelling shadows sped by. The little American and the Dutchman hung against the black wall with a piston rod swinging tons of metal past their heads, and let a score of dark ghosts rush up the iron walk. The companion ladder loomed, creaking under the weight of unseen, scrambling bodies, not far from Scarlet's head.

"Get ready!" Scarlet flung low, steely words into Schneider's ear. "They won't see us. The ladder. We've got to rush it. Beat down the crew an' th' Malays. No shooting. Might hit the wrong man. Use your gun-butt. We'll scale that ladder an' get out—"

The Dutchman panted like a valve. "I am with you. But *Himmel!* Where—where can we go—"

"We've got to get up that ladder!" Scarlet snarled. "An' then get to the bridge-deck. Quick, Schneider! We've got to get to that woman's cabin—"

GET TO the bridge-deck. The woman's cabin. For the life of him the beery Islamahad planter could not guess why Scarlet must risk climbing that jammed companionway, only to dash for those cabins on the upper deck again. But Wilhelm Schneider had long ago given up trying to think. Vaguely he heard Scarlet's barked instructions, and he set out to follow with all the grim doggedness that had once sent such Hollanders as Von Tromp and Pieter van Hoole battling down that same Asian sea.

Von Tromp and Pieter van Hoole never waged such a battle as did Schneider while trailing the little American up that cycloning companion ladder in the roaring bowels of that rolling mail ship. It was black as sin on that swinging iron stairway. One minute Scarlet was hanging by his hands from the under side of the ladder. Next minute he was climbing the backs of a knotted-up scrabble of flailing maniacs. Schneider, squawking from the pain of his stabbed shoulder, clawed his way into the openings the curio-hunter tore for him.

As for Peter Scarlet, he never knew how he got through that screaming tangle of Malays and sailors to reach the top of the companion. Lady Luck. More than once his feet kicked nothing but black air while his fingers held on an invisible iron rung and unseen boots tramped on his fingers. And when the top of the engine room companion was reached the fight was worse. The hatch was jammed with Malays and knives. Knives more vicious than bullets in the dark. The stairway up out of that blattering engine room did not lead to Paradise. Most people thought hell was down. It occurred to Peter Scarlet they were wrong. Hell was up. The higher he and Schneider climbed the worse it got.

But at least there was a place to plant a man's feet. The little American curio-hunter planted his feet in the hatchway, and swung his automatic. Steel crunched hard against bone. *Whack! Smash!* Beard blowing, mad cries whistling out of his teeth, Scarlet beat about him with a fierce gun-butt. A Malay *kris* razored a slice from his elbow. Missiles whirled past his head. One raving hurricane where one couldn't see the hand before his face or the knife that struck at his eyes. But they were out of the engine room. Now they had a chance.

"You all right, Schneider?"

"Ja! Du Lieber Gott—"

"Let's go!"

THEY WENT. Scarlet went first, and the Dutchman went after him. Bumping, floundering, rolling, tumbling down that madhouse alleyway leading aft. Gunfire smashed in fusillades from the companion they had left. The Scotch skipper and his men were getting up that ladder, too. The Malays were starting to run in the corridor like chickens with their heads cut off.

Scarlet swore at the darkness, but his frenzied hands found the bulkhead he remembered. The iron barrier clanged open. Fresh air breezed in, and a patch of sky appeared through a port overhead, a square of indigo scattered with pale stars. Catching at Schneider's collar, Scarlet fairly yanked the Dutchman up the ladder.

"On deck, old man! We'll win now—"

Forward of the bridge the Malays were racketing. Two figures with rifles were on the bridge wing, training their guns on the fore-deck below. Scarlet panted: "The wheelmen. It's all right. They're holding the natives back. Won't see us."

The curio-hunter was right. The pilots did not see him as he led Schneider fast across the bridge-deck, down the line of cabins and into that cabin numbered Four. The little American and the Dutchman would have been worth seeing, too. Schneider was a quivering bulk, oggle-eyed in tattered rags. Scarlet's coat was in ribbons and the knee had been torn from one pant-leg and he limped where his bootheel had been shot away. Red threads of blood leaked from a gash in his temple and seeped to dye the corners of a beard that had once been white.

Shoving what was left of his fat friend into the cabin the woman had occupied, Scarlet leapt to follow. An uncanny laugh burst from his teeth. The Dutchman leaned, panting, against the door while Scarlet bounced around the cabin like a maniac. Sweat burst on Schneider's sagging face. The little American curio-hunter tore open the woman's parasol, kicked at her slippers, snatched the silk shawl from its hook and flung it at the washstand, sprang up on the empty bunk and grabbed the little native handbag down off the shelf and poured a shower of trinkets to the floor. Had the little curio-hunter gone mad? Certainly he gave an insane shout when he stooped and caught up a shiny object from that clutter of spilled trinkets.

Peter Scarlet clapped that shiny object into his pocket before Schneider could see what it was; then the curio-hunter leaned against the bunk and laughed and laughed. A ray of light seeping through the cabin door found a glow in Scarlet's larkspur eyes that was not nice to see. Sweat coasted down his gashed face as he laughed.

Wilhelm Schneider, the beery Dutch planter from Islama-had, did not laugh. Wilhelm Schneider was choking with fright. His three chins trembled like jelly, and the blood was like jell in his veins. *Ach Gott!* here was nothing amusing. This horrible ship off the Java coast. This devil's raft where a missionary had been murdered and a Moslem priest with black whiskers and brown eyes could vanish and throw knives and vanish again. Then the little curio-hunter could suddenly yell he knew where this Emperor of Death was, and the Scotch captain did not believe. The captain had ordered Scarlet killed and Scarlet had escaped within an inch of death; and now rioting, terrified Malays were trying to wreck the ship and the sailors might come along any minute now and shoot everybody full of red holes. And Peter Scarlet had come to this Oriental woman's cabin that meant nothing at all, and here he waited doubled up with awful mirth while death closed in on all sides.

CHAPTER IX

THE MADNESS OF PETER SCARLET

WILHELM SCHNEIDER STARED at his little friend, and his tongue turned to dough in his mouth. *"Himmel!* Scarlet! My friend, my friend, we are lost now—"

"We're saved, Schneider! Saved! I've got it! I've got it!"

"We must get out of here, Peter. Hide. Hide. Quick. Any minute now the big captain and his men will come—"

On the bridge-deck outside there was a sudden furious clamor. Hammering boots. Yells. Gunfire. Squalling. A Scotch voice loud as a horn. "We've got 'em. We've got the Malays bottled up. Hold 'em on that forward deck. Stand by, mates. Round up th' crew. Hold those Malays. Now by God! we'll find those other two. We'll get that little murderer—"

Peter Scarlet chuckled. "They're on the deck outside." Gliding to the cabin door, Scarlet opened it a half crack and peeped through. When he turned around he was grinning, and his

Gun spitting flame, Scarlet burst into the cabin

Lüger was tight in his fist. "They're there. The captain, crew an' all. And the woman." Scarlet's voice came like chiseled steel. "Cheer up, Schneider. I'm not insane. Stick with me. We're going out there and round up the killer with the beard. Get ready with your gun. I'm not mad, Schneider. But it's going to sound like madness before I'm through—"

Schneider blinked—but he followed after....

Nobody was more surprised than Captain Angus Burl with the red Scotch face and fuzzy sideburns. With the woman at his elbow and his wounded mate on the other side, the big skipper had been leaning over the bridge rail training his pistol on the deck where the Malays were milling like corralled cattle. Captain Angus Burl never saw the wild little figure that sprang from the stateroom, followed by the grotesque caricature of the Dutchman. Captain Burl was a little more than surprised when a cold gun-muzzle rammed into his neck-nape, and a metallic order snapped low at his ear.

"Don't turn around. Make a move an' you're deader than mud. Tell your crew up on th' monkey bridge that everything's O.K. Tell those pilots to throw down their rifles. Stop!" The last command was directed at the mate, who had made a half turn. "Look for'ard there or I'll drill you through the head. The woman, too. Keep her covered, Schneider. If she opens her mouth let her have it. Now, Cap'n Burl, do as I say. Tell your crew to go to th' starboard wing of th' bridge."

Cold fear and hate glittered in the skipper's eye right then, and icicles of perspiration wiggled down his spine. It was dark on that bridge-deck. The crew on the upper bridge couldn't see what had happened. The Scotchman had an impulse to scream a warning. But the gun-muzzle in his neck gave a savage shove.

"Hi, men, go to starboard!" Fury shook the skipper's tongue. "You pilots up there. Drop them rifles. It's all right!"

There was a shuffle on the monkey bridge. "Now move," Scarlet snarled. "Walk backwards. Into this cabin here. I've got you covered. The three of you. Keep a bead on 'em, Schneider." Scarlet gave a thrust with his automatic. "Wait, Cap'n Burl. Lean over that rail an' yell down to those Malays. Tell 'em to quiet down. Tell 'em the Emperor of Death has been captured—"

STRANGE ABOUT panic. The skipper's voice barked hoarse through the darkness, and the natives on the deck below went quiet as if throttled by a monstrous hand. The Scotch master mariner of the Asian mail packet looked as if he'd been throttled, too. Peter Scarlet could have laughed at the red face with the fuzzy sideburns. But the rage reflected in those hard, sea-sharp eyes had to be stifled. Nothing for it but to obey the little curio-hunter's order. Nursed along by the guns of Scarlet and the Dutchman, the skipper, the mate and the woman made a slow backward march, back from the rail, back across the tilting deck, back into the open cabin door of stateroom Number Four.

Scarlet made a leap to knock the skipper's gun from his fingers, at the same time giving the mate a push. The woman made a quick glide, but Schneider's automatic drove her backwards into the cabin, and there was nothing for the mate to do but follow. Feet braced in the cabin door, Scarlet covered the three with his gun. "Stand quiet, all of you."

The only sound in the darkness was a steamy breathing. A slam as the curio-hunter kicked shut the door. "Now, Schneider, that lamp over the washstand—" A match flaring in a pudgy, cupped palm that quivered. Then amber light flooded from the cabin lamp.

It was a strange little scene. Schneider, fat, panting, pop-eyed, holding the lamp with shaky fingers. Scarlet against the door, battered and bleeding, fisting a steady gun. The wounded mate, the mouthing Scotch sea captain and the gold-skinned, veiled woman lined up along the wall.

"It won't go, you fiend!" The skipper voiced a raven-like croak. His Adam's apple gulped in his throat. Defiance glittered in his hard eyes, but his face was the color of something found under a stone. "You can't shoot us. No! You kill us an' my crew will get you sure as the devil! If you kill—" He stopped, panting furiously.

"Nobody's going to be killed," Peter Scarlet snapped, "until the police get ready to do it. Then it will be an execution. The police will execute the murderer who goes by the name of The Emperor of Death Who Wears The Beard! Cap'n Burl, you called to the frightened Malays an' told 'em The Emperor of Death had been captured. That's the truth. The Emperor of Death, the criminal sought by the police of six colonies, the assassin who slew a score of victims, followed me on this boat, killed the missionary, ran up here and chucked the costume of a Moslem priest overboard, then ducked below and threw knives at me—that murderer is now facing my automatic!"

The wounded mate gave a gasp. The veiled woman swayed and shot a terrified glance around her. Captain Angus Burl exhaled a rusty curse. Schneider wheezed and jiggled the lamp.

"Who"—the Scotch skipper's voice seemed to echo up out of a deep well, "who do you think the assassin is, you—"

IT WAS stifling in that swaying cabin. Hot. The little American curio-hunter's words dropped like metal pellets through the stricken atmosphere. "I'll tell you who it is. It's the person who walked around rigged up like a Moslem priest, flashing a big turban and a crimson mantle and a bright ring so's everybody would notice, an' petting a long black beard that you couldn't miss seeing. It's the one who overheard me say I was goin' to the smoke room at eight-thirty, an' ran down there an' stabbed the missionary, thinkin' it was me. This killer with big brown eyes couldn't see very well in the dim light of the smoking saloon. Queer, come to think of it. After all, a normal eye wouldn't have mistaken the missionary for me at close range. The murderer, it seemed, had bad vision. What was wrong with those big brown eyes, eh? Why, those nice big brown eyes were filled with belladonna or some tricky Asian drug which made 'em big an' changed their real color.

"When I guessed *that* I could see a little clearer, myself. You bet I could! I could see the killer dashin' up here into a cabin, ripping off the priest costume to heave it overside, then washing the belladonna away to make the eyes normal again, and jumping into another costume. Yeh. That's why there wasn't any Moslem priest to be found. Then the killer joins the chase an' runs below decks, sneaks topside again, chucks a knife into Schneider, hopin' to hit me. Why'd the killer want me dead? Because I'd snatched off the assassin's pet emerald ring, for one thing. But the blade hits Schneider. And when I gave chase the murderer hid by the after house and tossed some more daggers, pulling them out of the fresh costume."

Schneider's eyes widened.

Scarlet grimaced. "Those blades almost picked me off. But

the last one missed and I chased the killer around the stern. The killer seems to vanish. Same as the killer always seemed to vanish when the police ashore thought they were closing in. But the murderer is right there on that deck all the time. I should say so. And it was the ring business gave the killer away, after all. A ring leaves a mark on the finger that's been wearing it. The hand wearin' the ring gets tanned up, but the place where the ring was isn't sunburned, an' there's liable to be a faint white circle where the ring was on the finger—"

THE EYES of Captain Angus Burl were like polished stones. "Mark where a ring was. Priest costume chucked overboard. Belladonna in the eyes. A bloody good story. But where the devil is a man around with a black beard like that priest had growin' on his jaw. I suppose you'll say now they was false whiskers, eh? But you can't get away with it! You said before you *pulled them hairs out by the roots—*"

"So I did," said Peter Scarlet with a savage chuckle, "so I did. Pulled 'em out by the roots for certain." A harsh laugh sawed from his teeth. Reaching into a pocket, he fished to light a long silken black hair. "There's one of 'em. Look close an' you'll see the root on the end of it, an' a little chunk of skin, too. And now watch this." Scarlet held the long black hair to the point of his chin. All eyes were on that silken, ghastly black thread of hair. The thing fell almost to his knees.

"What the devil," snarled the skipper, "does that nonsense prove?" Captain Burl's face was a red cartoon of fury. His breath came in enraged gasps.

Peter Scarlet snarled, too. "You saw the priest, eh? Well, the priest's black beard fell to the chest, but it didn't fall to the knees! This black hair is a foot longer than the priest's chin whiskers, see! Apparently it was yanked out of the killer's chin. By the roots. But it wasn't yanked out of the killer's chin after all!"

Scarlet's voice went so low that the group which stood like a wax tableau in that cabin had to listen to hear. And they listened, too. "How," Scarlet whispered, "could I yank a hair from a black beard on a chin, and yet not have the hair come out of that chin at all? Crazy, isn't it? Believe me, I thought I was mad when I got the drift of this. But I had a hunch, an' now I've got proof. An' I found that proof right here in this woman's cabin, th' last place in the world this Emperor of Death Who Wears The Beard thought anybody'd look for it!"

Once more Scarlet delved in a pocket. This time he brought out in his palm a shiny object that glinted in his hand. The object Schneider had seen him pluck from the scatter of trinkets on the floor. A little black metal vial.

"Here's my proof, Cap'n Burl. This little bottle. Some more tricky Asian drug. Eye-wash? Not this time. But *dye-wash!*" With a magican-like gesture, the little curio-hunter uncorked the vial, and poured a drop of liquid on the long black hair. The tiny drop of liquid traveled down the hair like a diamond traveling down a thread. You could have heard the noise of that moving liquor-drop in the stifled cabin, then. For the long black hair was turning color. Turning blonde. Turning to a fine thread of gleaming bronze!

"YAAAH!" THE scream came so loud and sudden as to stun the men in that cabin. A golden, gauzy-veiled shadow shot across the cabin floor like a breath of wind. A tiger never sprang faster than that woman sprang. An orang never whipped out a quicker hand. Fast as a flash the woman hurled herself at Scarlet; snatched for his unready gun. Thrown over backwards, Scarlet crashed against the door. The door flew outward with a splintering smash, snapping off the hinges. Slim ankles tripped on Scarlet's kicking boots, and the woman toppled with a shriek, as the vial of dye-wash sailed from Scarlet's palm, scattering a tiny shower.

It was queer how the woman kept on tumbling, with that poisonous liquid in her eyes. The ship gave a roll and she was against the rail, screaming; and as suddenly she was gone.

They got to the rail yelling, but too late. The last thing they saw was a flourish of bronze hair spreading like some strange sea-moss in the froth of a combing roller. The roller broke with a boom, and that was all.

"I'll keep the emerald ring," said Scarlet evenly, "as my reward."

THE SCOTCH captain's cabin was better. There were wicker chairs and three bottles of Johnny Walker to be had. A bottle for the captain. A bottle for Wilhelm Schneider. And a bottle for the little American curio-hunter.

In the east the sun was rising in a sky of solid gold, and Java, lying to starboard, was a dark line of blue under gentle pink clouds.

"But I'm damned," said Captain Angus Burl, setting down a glass that wasn't empty for the first time in his life, and glaring at Peter Scarlet. "I certainly am."

Wilhelm Schneider, the beery Dutch planter from Islama-had, mopped his three chins and nodded. *"Ach Gott!* So am I."

The little American curio-hunter lay back in his chair and smiled. "And so was I," he agreed. "The thing had me stumped. Don't wonder the skipper figured I was the Emperor of Death right down to th'very last. Somebody had to be, and his idea was as reasonable as any. When the Moslem priest vanished under our noses and the charming Oriental lady walked out of that last cabin last night I thought Asia had gone to my head. And when the knife-thrower vanished around the stern I thought sure I was off. But it's easy when you figure about the woman. First, she came aboard and went into that cabin of hers. Then she stepped out as the Moslem holy man and took the cabin next Schneider's. Then she killed the missionary, fled topside into her cabin, kicked out of the Moslem rig, heaved it overboard and was ready for us with a smile when we knocked on her door. With that drug out of her eyes she saw she'd killed the wrong man. She trailed the skipper into the hold, doubled back and threw the knives. When I chased her around the after house all she had to do was come back on her trail and meet me calm and nice as you please.

"She wanted us to think the mysterious priest had bounced overside. That's why, when she spotted the turban, she showed it to us. Take our minds off the chase and fill us with confusion. And when the skipper accused me it gave her a real break. She plays into the captain's hand by telling how she saw a body go splash."

Scarlet hoisted a drink and grinned. "It was when she pointed her hand under my nose that I had the first glimmer. The lantern light fell straight on her hand. That's when I spotted the place a ring had been. Then the whole thing came clear like a rocket going through my head. But how the devil could I prove? Cap'n Burl was going to lock me in irons, an' the killer would get away sure. I just had to get into her cabin for a look around. And when I did get up there and discover that nice little vial of dye-wash I knew I had the goods on the Emperor of Death, and the Emperor of Death knew it, too."

"But shades of Friedrich Wilhelm!" Schneider exploded. "The ring. The drugged eyes. The priest costume. *Ja.* But how about the—"

"The beard that came out by the roots?" Peter Scarlet smiled softly. "Easy. No wonder the Emperor of Death pulled so many quick get-aways. All she did was dye her hair black and let it down and fasten it with stickum or something along her chin. With a turban covering the top of her head it looked as if the hair grew out of her face. When I yanked that hair loose it actually came out of her scalp. She fled to her cabin, washed the black out of her hair with dye-remover, and did it up into a beautiful bronze mop of curls. Now who in the world would have ever suspected the Emperor of Death as a woman? A beautiful woman, too."

Scarlet sighed plaintively.

"But there's an old proverb that the bumboat man at Balanipa once told me when I pricked my finger on a stem and then a bee flew out of the flower and stung me in the ear. 'Beware the thorn,' he told me. 'Ten thousand times beware the rose.' And she certainly was a rose—"

ABOUT THE AUTHOR

AS A GUEST speaker at Pulpcon in Dayton, Ohio in July, 1986, I played the old Q. and A. game. I believe the opening of that game makes a good beginning for the present discussion of my fiction writing for the pulps.

Q. How and when did my fiction writing begin?

A. I have in my files the initial effort—a book entitled *The Devul and the Knight* [sic] written age five, hand-printed, hand-illustrated and hand-bound, price one cent (two copies, one remainder). The "K" circumflexed over the "night" was inserted by a brother ten years my senior. From the penny profit (from a sale within the family), I purchased a Mary Jane—taffy wrapped around a glob of peanut butter. Um.

Q. Then?

A. Shortly thereafter, I wrote, hand-printed, hand illustrated and hand-bound *Hawk Eye the Indian Boy* (two copies, price one cent, one remainder) which bought me another Mary Jane.

Q. And?

A. There followed a production entitled *The Sheriff of Red Roach Ranch*. ("Roach" was the spelling of my wicked older brother when I asked him if "Rock" was spelled with two "Ks." No matter.) I copied the spelling "Sheriff and "Ranch" from a book I was reading. Again, the one cent sale (leaving one remainder) paid for another Mary Jane.

Thus I conceived a notion.

Born was the idea that by writing I could eat.

That idea served as an apothegm for my subsequent career as a writer—a ruling not invariably a truism. As it eventuated there were times when I had Thanksgiving dinner at bottom of the totem pole at a hot dog stand.

However, I wrote many yarns for my high school magazine-an effort that caused an English teacher to suggest I submit a fiction effort to a magazine. Not overly optimistic, I knew I couldn't compete in a try for that day's top, the *Saturday Evening Post.* So I picked a pulp—*NorthWest Stories.* Luck! A check for $40.00! And a request for another story. This first story, "The Duel," would appear in the September 1926 issue.

That did it.

It was summertime, and I'd been a temporary P.O. employee peddling mail on a route on Long Island. With a high school buddy similarly employed, who shared room and board. And I had just carried a very heavy parcel-post package addressed to a "Tillie Tisswisser," 8,001 some local avenue at the end of the line. After lugging it an extra half mile, I discovered there was no such address. Belatedly suspicious, I pried open one corner of the package and exposed a cinder block. Which my pal had wrapped and mailed with a slew of cancelled stamps.

That would have done it if my check hadn't come that day with $40.00. "I quit! I just made a fortune!" I told them at the P.O. where I dumped the cinder block. (And I got even with my buddy by ducking out of our boarding house by letting my suitcase out of our bedroom window on a clothes line and leaving him stuck with the rent.)

Anyway, the $40.00 check started me on what eventuated as a career, writing for *Action Stories, Argosy, Short Stories* and *Adventure,* for such astute editors as Jack Byrne, Don Moore and, after the war (World War II), Burroughs Mitchell and Bud Hart. Of whom I still see Bud Hart—the others no longer among those present.

World War II pretty much killed most of the now extinct pulps. From paper shortage? I can't say. But many pulp writers faded away during the war. Among them, one of the best. Frederick Faust ("Max Brand"). I'm not certain, but I believe he may have been killed at Anzio.

If one finds some astonishing names among the early pulp editors some of the writers are equally surprising. In the early *Argosy-All Story.* Mary Roberts Rinehart, Octavus Roy Cohen, Zane Gray, E. Phillips Oppenheim, John Buchan. (Buchan, who wrote "The Thirty-Nine Steps," became Governor-General of Canada.)

Theodore Roscoe

ONE OF the questions often asked me is how did I happen to write about an old veteran yarn-spinner who spun yarns about his service in the French Foreign Legion. In North Africa back in the early '30s I encountered on a street in Casablanca this old-time Legionnaire with hashmarks up to his elbow. He agreed to talk over wine at a *brasserie.*

He didn't wear the classic old-time Legion uniform-the button-back blue overcoat, white trousers, blue cummerbund, heavy desert-boots called *brodequins.* He wore an old artilleryman's outfit. But the square-brim *kepi* with the gold torch insignia was Legion.

Questioning him in my limping French, and struggling to comprehend his metaphors, I got a *formidable* story. Aside from obvious hyperbole and manifest adjectives, some of it was perhaps true.

Here was my prototype for Thibaut Corday. Which, of course, wouldn't be his right name. You could enlist in the Legion under any name you chose, and since his right name was Hyacinth Rastagouch, he chose Corday for what is called a *nom de guerre.* Which became your official name as a "Stepson of France." Meaning you couldn't be extradited for a crime committed elsewhere—a fact, it was said contributed to the enlistment of numerous criminals using an alias. Who knows?

Because Frenchmen can't enlist in the French Legion, I had Corday say he was a Belgian. Or was it a Swiss? Anyway, the teller of my story attributed to Corday good English, partly translated.

Since his yarns were obviously mixtures of fact and fiction, I never presumed they would be taken seriously by the reader. And was surprised when several critics wrote to tell me the military tactics in this or that Corday tale were hokum. They were so intended to sound.

Incidentally, some Legion veterans in New York voted me an honorary member of the Veterans of the French Foreign Legion.

Actually, I never saw the Legion in combat. At a Legion H.Q. back in Sidi Bel Abbes, I was querying one of the officers. Apparently he thought I was planning to enlist. He shook his head at me with the comment: *"Discipline terrible!"* They followed the old rule, *"March qu creve."* "March or die." If a Legionnaire fell out, exhausted, in a Sahara march, they sent a sharpshooter back to kill him, and spare him from torture by desert tribesmen. But the Legionnaires I saw in action weren't risking their lives.

In Europe back then there was a saying. When the English conquer a country they build a custom house. The Germans build a fort. The French build a road. Back then (the '30s) the Legionnaires I saw in action were covered with not-very-glamorous dust, wielding picks and shovels building a road. Some of them in barracks slept in cots with the cot-legs in cans filled with water, to defeat scorpions. Their pay, if I recall correctly, afforded them a daily bottle of *pinard* (cheap red wine). Nothing so intriguing, colorful and lively as in such novels as *Beau Geste*.

So don't join the French Foreign Legion today. You'd get a plain khaki uniform, and risk only being bored to death.

Still, you'd learn one thing. Watch them, if chance occurs, on parade in France or on TV. There's no military outfit anywhere that can out-march their particular step.

ASIDE FROM the Foreign Legion, I most enjoyed writing for *Action Stories* a series about an adventurer named Peter Scarlet. There were at least 14 Peter Scarlet stories, beginning with "Jungle Joker" in the May 1927 issue of *Action Stories*. Other favorites were a tale entitled "On Account of a Woman" (*Adventure*, January 1936) and a tale for *Argosy*, "The Voodoo Express" (October 10,1931).

On another tack, I enjoyed writing a series for *Argosy* titled "Four Corners," which began with "He Took Richmond" in the June 5, 1937 issue of *Argosy*. These were adventures experienced by a youngster whose uncle was Sheriff in a small town about 100 miles from New York. One of the early Four Corners stories was "I Was the Kid With the Drum" (October 30, 1937)—a murder mystery. They used to have a kid aid the drummer by carrying in a parade the front end of a big base drum (guess where the body was concealed in a hurry by the murderer in this case). Of course, the drum seemed heavier than usual. And the drum-beat seemed more of a thump than the usual vibratory boom. The kid in the story didn't get it. But anyway the murderous drummer discovered he'd killed the wrong person.

In another "Four Corners" tale, I had a thief change his money into coins—loot he could bury in a well. Okay? But when he went back to safely get and spend this big bag of coins, he was trapped by the fact the silver dollars all bore the same date—the date of the robbery.

In one of my favorite Four Corners stories, "Frivolous Sal" (*Argosy*, July 17, 1937), the small town gentry were worried because it was rumored the young woman, so named (after a popular song), kept a diary. Fruitless efforts were made to get hold of it. In the end? Try to guess it.

I had a lot of fun writing "The Head," which appeared in *Short Stories*, December 10, 1932. As a stringer reporter, I had gone to Panama to investigate rumors of "White Indians" in the remote interior near the Colombian border. At a bar in Cristobal I asked the bar-keep if he'd heard of these Indians. Overhearing my query, a bar-fly character asked if I was interred in Jiboro Indians—the tribe that, through a mysterious process, boned, cured and somehow shrank human heads to the size of a base-ball. (Origin of the term "head-shrinker" for a psychologist.) The bar-fly said he had one to sell, and produced what appeared to be a much-shrunken human head. As the Jiboro Indians actu-ally beheaded their enemies and with incredible artsy-crafty skill created such curiosities, I was interested in the specimen handed me by the bar-fly. Ah! Only $300.00.

But the bartender, behind his hand, winked at me a negative signal. I didn't buy the head.

When the bar-fly indignantly took off with his allegedly shrunken head, the bartender advised me it was a fake, a monkey head fixed up to look human.

Later I saw an authentic shrunken head on display in another bar.

When World War II put an end to my pulp efforts, by good luck I sold *Only in New England*—a novel I'd intended for *Argosy*—to Scribner's. Surprisingly, it made the Literary Guild Book of the Month.

Thereafter, I wrote two Navy histories—*U.S. Submarine Oper-ations, World War II* (1949) and *U.S. Destroyer Operations, World War II* (1953) which were published by the Naval Institute at Annapolis (and are still on the market). I also wrote *This is Your Navy* (1950) for service reading. This was followed by *The Web of Conspiracy* (1959), about the Lincoln assassination, which became a *DuPont Show of the Month* on TV in 1961. Of which, with a great deal of help from my devoted wife, Rosamond, got me going again in fiction.

Today I can't recall what some of these tall tales written 50 years ago were about. Maybe I should have written some of them under an assumed name. But when I wrote them I felt I should take my lumps if, compared to many of early *Argosy's* great writers, my efforts proved mediocre. And on the other hand, if some drew plaudits, I'd like to take a bow in person.

Brave, no?

THE ARGOSY LIBRARY ™

SERIES 6 INCLUDES:

* BRAND * CUMMINGS * BRENT *
FARLEY * AUBREY * ROSCOE *
* GIESY & SMITH *
* LAMB * FOOTNER *
* McCULLEY *

THE BEST FICTION
FROM THE FRANK
A. MUNSEY LINE